The GuTuesday

THE GURKHA AND
THE LORD OF TUESDAY

SAAD Z. HOSSAIN

A TOM DOHERTY ASSOCIATES BOOK

NEW YORK

THE GURKHA AND THE LORD OF TUESDAY

Copyright © 2019 by Saad Z. Hossain

Cover art by Eric Nyquist
Cover design by Christine Foltzer

Edited by Jonathan Strahan

A Tor.com Book
Published by Tom Doherty Associates
120 Broadway
New York, NY 10271

www.tor.com

Tor® is a registered trademark of
Macmillan Publishing Group, LLC.

ISBN 978-1-250-20910-8 (ebook)
ISBN 978-1-250-20911-5 (trade paperback)

First Edition: August 2019

The Gurkha and the Lord of Tuesday

Chapter One

The Long Release

Drip. Drip. Twenty years of ice melt, wearing away long-buried boulders, reveals a sudden right angle of stone, a geometric peculiarity in the otherwise pristine geology of the Kanchenjunga, most sacred of mountains, five conjoined peaks in the heart of the Himalayas, forbidden to climbers, one of the few remaining secret places of the Earth.

Twenty years of water dripping against a slightly misshapen, bulbous skull. Melek Ahmar, the Lord of Mars, the Red King, the Lord of Tuesday, Most August Rajah of Djinn, asleep for millennia, woken once more by the vagaries of water and stone, found his eyes covered in grit. His mouth, too. He spat out dust and gagged.

His sarcophagus was plain stone, a monolith hewn with crude chisels, his body dumped irreverently inside, the lid forced shut by mortar and spells, constructs of the field produced by some master rune worker, almost as if it were a prison rather than a comfortable resting place.

Which, in fact, it was, of course. Melek Ahmar had not gone to sleep willingly. Well, as willingly as anyone hit on the back of the head with a mace. As far as he could remember, it hadn't even been in battle. He had been drinking. Some brave soul had crept up behind him and bashed his skull in. It felt like yesterday. He tried to reach back and feel for the lump, but of course his limbs were constrained, first by the coffin-like stricture of the stone and then by the shroud itself, which still retained some potency, its strands of power wrapping him in spider silk.

And this incessant dripping. Was it some devilish torture devised by his enemies? No. It was fucking natural snowmelt. They'd buried him and then just forgotten about him. It was insupportable.

He searched for the field, the ubiquitous power source running through the universe, accessible, *detectable* only to the djinn, the foundation of their superiority. All djinn could manipulate the field, distort and bend it within their circumference, use it to change the very nature of matter and energy. The breadth and strength of the distortion sphere varied from djinn to djinn; some were weak, wavering things. Melek Ahmar's was the size of a small mountain.

He flexed his distortion, and felt the power coalesce into something almost solid. The spells meant to neuter him were in tatters. They broke apart like cobwebs, sticky and feather-light on his skin. That was disturbing. Spells were constructs in the field itself, a sort of runic engineering, tied off and meant to last for the ages. Only time ruined spells. The stone was spongy too, like cottage cheese, full of holes. Time did that to stone too. Time and water. How the fuck long had he been asleep?

He gathered his strength. This time, when he flexed his arms, everything gave way in a gratuitously dramatic manner. The sarcophagus flew apart, embedding the mountain with shards of runic stone, and the spell-work shredded, the inky lines of the construct disintegrating, reaffirming to Melek Ahmar that he was the mightiest of djinn, the august, the puissant. It was vaguely disturbing that no one was in attendance to witness such feats. One did not like to brag. If great feats of strength were entirely unwitnessed, it was almost as if they had never happened, which was a shame. Where were the bards?

Melek Ahmar stood up on shaky legs, and found that he had to support himself with the distortion field. His damn legs had atrophied. He looked down at his calves and found that they had inexplicably shrunk to half their mighty girth. His biceps, his dear, beloved biceps, good lord, they were barely bigger than his forearms. At maximum flex! He couldn't even see the veins properly. At least his gut had shrunk. How long?? And not a sentinel in sight. Not even a raven or a magic frog or something.

Had they actually *forgotten* about him?

His mood worsening by the minute, he stumbled out of the crevice and started the long journey down.

Four days later, he was still hobbling down the mountain, and getting progressively crabbier. His body was emaciated to the point of ridiculousness, and his distortion field wasn't much better, a shriveled-up thing that could barely float him off the ground. He had killed a mountain goat and used its skin to make shoes, so now he smelled of rotten goat, which was further humiliation to a djinn of his address. Worse, the bits of the shroud he was using as a sarong were rotting off with each step, so that now half his mighty genitalia were flopping around in an ungainly way. He was, of course, endowed with the stature and girth befitting a king, but the cold mountain air and the god knows how many years of hibernation *was* bound to take a toll, wasn't it? How was he supposed to ravage unsuspecting Humes in this kind of state? He was irritated enough to flatten mountains. Which he had done in the past, of course. Anyone remember the great peaks of Lemuria? Exactly. Those were the fucking days.

Ambling along in a fugue of pleasant memories, he almost missed the small, unassuming Gurkha man lounging on a rock, an oldish fellow with an unusually impressive moustache, a thing of oiled, clipped beauty, and if it was a little sparse, the upward curl of the tips were symmetrical and precisely pointed.

Not unnaturally, this man was sitting on the rock twirling said moustache, a hand-rolled cigarette clamped between his teeth, as yet unlit. He was clothed simply, and did not seem particularly disturbed by the bitter cold. There was a cheery ease about him, as if he owned these mountains and was inspecting them at his leisure.

Melek Ahmar, almost atop him, stopped and stretched out his arms.

"Tremble before me, Hume! I am Melek Ahmar, the Grand Mark of the Tigris, Enlil of the Ziggurats, the Wrecker of Mountains, the Lord of Tuesday! I have returned!"

"Bhan Gurung." The Gurkha flashed a smile, teeth white against his leathery brown skin. He struck out his bare hand.

"Ahem, yes, well." Melek Ahmar, nonplussed, found himself shaking hands with this pathetic, title-less Hume. There was something compelling about his insouciant grin.

"Want a nut?" Gurung asked.

Upon closer inspection Melek Ahmar found that this reprobate was in fact shelling pistachios with his curved kukri and eating them. The rock he was sitting on was littered with the shells. It was a disgrace. However, Melek Ahmar was starving.

"Are they salted?" he asked.

"What kind of criminal salts pistas?" Gurung asked, incensed.

"Quite right," the Lord of Tuesday said. "Well, move over then."

It wasn't quite what he had had in mind, his first day back among the Humes. On the other hand, the chill had receded a bit in the sunlight, the pistachios were sweet, and this mustachioed fellow was handy with the kukri.

"You're a good Hume," he said to Gurung, in between mouthfuls. "I had sworn to dismember the first one I found, but no. Behold my awesome mercy. I will stay my hand. But sooner or later, the urge to decapitate someone will become unbearable, be warned."

Gurung smiled. "I know just where to find many people needing decapitation. But first, a nap."

~

Gurung lived in a hovel attached to a cave. This was actually a fairly generous description. The cave was not one of those cathedral-like structures boasting nature's hidden majesty. It was more the sort of place where a starving runty bear kicked out of the bear clan might winter, nursing its wounds and promising dire vengeance on its fellows come spring.

The King of Mars, used to the palaces of Luxor, the forgotten luxuries of Gangaridai, the sheer effrontery of ancient Lhasa, was most unimpressed.

"You live *here*?"

"The entire Kanchenjunga is my house," Gurung said loftily. "This is just where I keep my things."

"You live here. In this shack. Attached to a hole in the mountain."

"You crawled out of a stone box, you said."

Melek Ahmar could not dispute this fact, and he was too weary to fully express the scale of his previous grandeur and auctoritas, so he merely glowered. It wasn't a particularly satisfying glower either, because it just seemed to roll off Gurung.

"Look, come inside and have some tea," Gurung said.

Ensconced together in the cave, where it was warmer, with the kettle on some kind of heating device, Melek Ahmar had to admit this was an improvement on the bitter outdoors. Gurung had quite a snug setup. There were a lot of humming noises, and a little metal box was running around aimlessly on the floor, and magic pictures were flickering along one wall. Melek was a bit disconcerted, but his natural bravado made him lean back and accept it in the manner befitting a king. Obviously this Gurung was a Nephilim sorcerer of some sort, but what a peculiar magic; he could see no disturbance in the field, and for that matter, no purpose to the spells either.

"So, Nephilim, you must be the guardian of my prison after all," he said, after drinking some tea. "Crafty of them, to keep such an unassuming jailor. Still, your puny frame must hide some strength. Be warned, I can dismember you with a twitch of my finger, even in this weakened state. I have stayed my hand, only because I have taken a liking to your ferocious ugliness."

"I am not a Nephilim or a sorcerer," Gurung said. "Nor was I waiting for you, ancient one."

"What are these things then?" Melek Ahmar demanded, pointing at the images.

"Oh. Yes. How long exactly have you been asleep?"

"Sometime after Memmion the Crass and Horus Light Bringer destroyed Gangaridai and the High King turned the world to ice. I mean I don't remember any of it because I was blind drunk at the time, but I would have been there otherwise. Those old boys begged me to join the war. Because I had the Mace of One Hit, you know? Get anyone with the MOH, and it's game over."

"None of those words have any meaning to me."

"Hmm. Where are all the kings of djinn?"

"Not many kings around these days."

"What about those Nephilim in Egypt building the triangle pointy things?"

"Pyramids. They're called pyramids."

"Yes, I definitely remember those. Biggest waste of time ever. That bitch Davala was inciting them to do it, for some convoluted purpose, no doubt. Anyway, how long ago was that?"

"That was like five or six thousand years ago."

"What about those Greeks? That Menelaus fellow who made a big stink about his wife . . . I remember those savages used to make a good wine."

"That was over three thousand years ago . . ."

"That's not good." Melek Ahmar frowned. *Four thousand years asleep? Three thousand? That was excessive even for djinn.*

"And this sorcery?" he asked, pointing at the moving pictures.

"It's technology. The Virtuality. Shows us what's happening everywhere. It's all small machines. We've become very good at making small machines. There are millions of microscopic, semi-organic machines in the air right now, going in and out of our bodies, scrubbing the air, getting rid of disease, fighting with other, hostile nano-stuff. It was the only way, they said, to save the planet. Nanotech. We live in clouds of it, we make it in our bodies, and if there's enough of the good kind in the air, we live, and if not, we die. It's the price of being citizens."

"Is that the buzzing noise?"

Gurung pointed at two sleek-looking boxes. "Nanotech fabricator. Solar battery for power. It's creating an artificial little microclimate, because there's only one of me here, so not enough for equilibrium. It blows the good stuff around the house. Keeps me alive, supposedly. Used to be a time when you could walk around outside. Still can, most days, but when the bad wind blows, you'll be dead in an hour. Of course, in the city, they have enough nannites in the air to actually create real climate conditions, so they can engineer clouds and rain and clear skies on demand."

Melek Ahmar grunted. "No little machines in the sky can hurt me." He was fairly sure about that. Still, it seemed as if these Humes had somehow mastered weather magic.

"Of course, ancient one."

"There is a city, you mentioned."

"Kathmandu Incorporated, in a valley almost two hundred kilometers from here. It's the only one that survived in these parts."

"Is it a great city?"

"A most beautiful one," Gurung said. He waved his hand, and the images on the wall flickered to life in three dimensions, a topography of spires and pagodas, embedded with towers sculpted in sinuous shapes. Sleek pod-like cars floated in the sky, either from cables or some kind of maglev, or even the holy grail of anti-grav. The skies overhead were a clear, austere blue, not a smudge of pollution anywhere. The voiceover descriptions meant little to Melek, but Gurung's pictures were impressive.

"Humph," Melek Ahmar said. This place reminded him of ancient Gangaridai, the first city of djinn, now gone from this world. Of course, Gangaridai had been superior. Still. What luck that the first city he should find would be this wondrous, fragile thing ripe for crushing? "This city will do."

"Do for what?" Gurung smiled.

"I am a king. It appears all of my subjects are missing," Melek Ahmar said. "I require worshippers, courtly followers, and sycophants. Also, a harem and bodyguards and moderately loyal drinking companions. This Kathmandu city shall bow down before me! I will rule once again."

"Of course, Your Eminence."

"Who is the king of this city?"

"We have no kings, Worshipful Lord."

"Ah, you are republican scum then. Anarchists."

"You know republicans?"

"We *invented* republicans," Melek Ahmar said. "That arch anarchist Memmion is the father of the movement. He started the great war in the first place, did you know that? They always blame Horus, but it was his big bastard sword cutting someone in two that started the damn thing. I hated that fucker, but he was a magnificent bastard when drunk. I can't tell you how many times we got fish faced and blasted apart entire mountains. That big lake where the Nile comes from? That was us. I'm the rightful father of the Nile, I am. Who rules below, then? Some scummy council of merchants? It's always scummy merchants."

"The city has a perfect ruler," Gurung said. "Universally hailed."

"A perfect tyrant? There is no such thing. Other than myself, perhaps."

"It is not conscious, so it wants nothing. It thinks at the speed of light. It can see and hear everything, even your thoughts most of the time. It keeps score of everything, no matter how great or small."

"This is a riddle. Oh, it's the Sphinx! The answer is always the Sphinx!" Melek Ahmar said.

"No, Great Lord of Tuesday," Gurung said, puzzled. "It is Karma."

Chapter Two

The City Below

The next morning, Gurung brought out a cardboard box. Inside was a tiny jar and a polished black object, the size and shape of a spinal bone. The jar was filled with a gel-like fluid, and embedded inside was a very faint, very small jellyfish creature made of luminescent thread, almost alive, radiating a disconcerting vitality. Melek Ahmar stared at these objects, nonplussed.

"PMD," Gurung said, pointing at the black bone. "Personal medical device. This was attached to my spine before I took it out." He lifted his shirt and showed a scar in the small of his back. He shook the jar, making the jellyfish undulate. "This is called an Echo. It's implanted in your brain when you're seventeen, eighteen. It grows there, afterward becomes a part of your mind. I took it out. Almost every person has these two augments. I told you, we are now a technological marvel. The PMD runs your body and keeps you healthy. It also makes the nanotech that humans contribute to maintain the environment. The tax, so to speak. The Echo lets you interface with the Virtuality directly from your brain, so all communication, and virtual interaction, is telepathic. It also lets you interact with physical services like transportation, homes, food vat machines. People who refuse these two augments are recidivists."

"Like us," Melek Ahmar said. He tapped the jar. The jellyfish was oddly mesmerizing.

"We will go to the city soon. I am warning you that without these, Karma will not recognize us as citizens, and we will be closely monitored. Please act accordingly."

"I will act as I see fit," Melek Ahmar said. "However, I will stay my hand until I can judge what force this city can bring to bear against me. Why have you removed these wonders from your body?"

"These things . . ." Gurung said. "Karma keeps score with these things. She can read your mind, almost. I was cast out of the city, so why should I keep their badges inside my body?"

"You are like Memmion, little man." Melek Ahmar clapped Gurung on the back approvingly. "You refuse to bend the knee. No djinn would submit to this indignity either."

"There are djinn in the city, Great One," Gurung said.

"We will find them, and I will lead them to glory!" Melek Ahmar said. "But first, I will study this Virtuality. I have four thousand years of gossip to catch up on."

~

The road to the city was paved and winding. In years past, before the air became poisoned and untenable, a stream of tourists, mountaineers, and pilgrims had come this way. Humans at that time had been largely rooted to the ground. This troubled Melek Ahmar. The air had once been the demesne of djinn and birds, and birds didn't count, for they were largely mindless. The sentience of the upper reaches had been represented solely by djinnkind. Now humans floated with invisible nanotech, zipped around on little pods, flew great distances on rockets. It was said they had reversed gravity completely in distant space stations. He understood these terms now, realized how far they had come in the last few thousand years. Of course, they had completely cocked up the planet, too. *And where are the djinn? Have we ceded the Earth completely? Has their technology out-jumped our magic? Unthinkable.*

They *no longer used* roads. All the roads of the world had somehow overnight become lifeless, filled with lonely machines plodding around, through billboards and abandoned rest stops slowly rusting. It was peculiar. And no one lived in the countryside. An invisible holocaust, forcing people to huddle in compact cities, resulting in nature slowly erasing the signs of humanity out here altogether. One would think nature had won this round, but Gurung assured him that the air was poisoned, that without nanotech living things could not thrive here and almost all large mammals were gone. Once they saw a misshapen goat with two heads to reinforce this point. Melek Ahmar did not care for nanotech or human disease. He ate both heads and then the rest of the goat too. Gurung found this amusing; the little Hume sat on the rock and watched, twirling his big knife, eating nuts. He seemed to have an inexhaustible supply.

There were no travelers on the road. Walking the trails was death. Gurung wore a mask and a little canister that produced puffs of emergency nanotech. Every inch of his body was covered with special fabric. He followed an internal chart of winds and currents, like Vasco de Gama hopping from island to island, stopping at oases of good air, skirting bad patches, so that their trip stretched into a week, then two, then three. It should have been an epic journey of adventure and self-discovery, but in reality it was just dull. Melek Ahmar would have barreled through, but he was slightly wrong-footed by this bizarre new world, and so he followed the little man, nursing his power, but his irritation grew, and by the time they reached the outskirts of the valley he was ready to blast someone into atoms.

When they finally reached the city at dawn, the djinn realized that Gurung had planned this approach with some care. The first view was stunning. The sun rose behind, and the city sparkled in tones of copper and gold, from domes and pagodas and metallic towers, from incredibly slender spires and crystal spheres that seemed to float above the land, and there was water flowing from the sky, and trees upside down, suspended from god knows what ... Kathmandu was beautiful, stunning, it was magic.

Melek Ahmar grunted after a moment and spat. He was the King of Mars. This much beauty simply irritated him.

"It is a wonder of the world, yes?" Gurung asked.

"Yes, wonderful," Melek Ahmar said. "I can imagine the little Humes strutting around like peacocks. I want to stamp on it and break open those floating spheres. I want to rip out those upside down trees and pick my teeth with them. We lived in cities once. I hated them." *Yes, and sadly on the day and night that cesspit Gangaridai finally disappeared, I was blind drunk and passed out in the ruins of Mohenjo Daro and so missed all the fun.*

Gurung smiled. He always smiled. *Was he a halfwit?*

They entered through the West Gate.

Chapter Three

The Punic Failsafe

Hamilcar Pande worked for Central Administration. He came from a bastardized offshoot of a Kshatriyan noble family, somehow crossed with Carthaginian blood, his mother some relict of ancient Punic glory, so that within him were the crossroads of most of history, the blood of warriors and explorers, and a distemper in some fold of his brain that made him restless and yearning.

No one was quite sure what he did, including himself. Central Admin itself was a strange place, because there wasn't really much to administer. The city was run by Karma, and Karma was not self-aware. Karma didn't care, she simply did her job, and did that damn well. Kathmandu ran without fear or failure. Central Admin was the failsafe, but what failsafe made up of meat could possibly deal with a situation where Karma *herself* failed? Could Hamilcar Pande make the trains run in the sky? No. Could he make water fall upward? No. Could he scrub from the air the evil nanotech the world shoveled at Kathmandu every day? No. Karma did this and everything else. Or rather, her subsystems did. Karma's main job was not running city systems. There were plenty of AI around the world doing just that, maintaining microclimes, running water, food, shelter. Karma did math. Her job was to keep score. *Of everything.*

Every so often, an aberration occurred, which disturbed Karma's vast mind. She had no sense of self, allegedly, so there was no emotional subtext to her disquiet. Still, Hamilcar could feel it, that light flutter along systems, which denoted something irregular. It was his job to investigate. No one had appointed him to this job, at least in his memory, but being of Puritanical nature, he hated sitting around doing nothing.

His previous attempts to help had rated approval from Karma. For that is what Karma did, of course, she rated the works, efforts, even the intentions of all her flock, and she awarded points for public service. She sifted through all the shit of humanity and she gave value, market value, and her judgment was beyond contest, for who in their right minds would argue with the vast computational power of Karma, whose creation was shrouded in mystery, whose systems could not be understood *even by other AI?*

And Karma wanted nothing, her systems were infallible, she was relentlessly fair, she predicted well beyond the ken of human understanding, and found the truth in actions and inventions that benefited the city in ways far removed from what mammalian logic or instinct could anticipate. Was she divine? Half of the city seemed to think so, yet in a laughing way, as if keeping pocket gods was now a birthright for men.

Kathmandu was rich, Karma made it richer beyond measure. Hamilcar yearned to be useful, to *do,* but he understood that his credo was hopelessly outdated. New philosophies had come to play these days, thoughts based on Hedonism and Epicureanism, ideas entirely necessary because there simply *wasn't* any work for all those Puritans hungry for salvation, nothing useful to do, no crops to grow, no factories to work, no armies to man, no roads to build, nothing manual, nothing intel-lectual, only a series of human interactions pandering to each other in turn. And when bodies could be healed at whim, when the brain could be played with on a molecu-lar level, why not search for pleasure, why not explore the absolute limits of excess? There were sybarites and dare-devils, madmen and savants, celebrities famous for being famous. Yet people like Hamilcar persisted, and so un-happiness persisted, that annoyance at becoming irrele-vant to the essential working of one's own society, until Karma came, Karma who tweaked the system and gave value and validation, who made people useful, because she could see far and wide into everyone and everything.

And so when Hamilcar felt her process list spike and flutter, he turned his Echo to the cameras, and took the feed from the western gate. Two men, waiting. They were wilderness people. Had they walked here? Karma had already scanned their bodies several times. Ah. They had no Echo, no PMD. No wonder they were invisible to most of her systems. They were trying to physically talk to the gate. These were primitives. Rare. Primitives had mostly died off during the first two decades of the Dissolution Era, before the necessity of microclimates had been fully accepted. Karma didn't like people without Echos. She couldn't read their minds.

Savages. One of them was actually wearing an animal skin. Yes. This deserved the full attention of Central Admin. Hamilcar Pande subvocalized a command, and his Echo sent a request for microdrone surveillance to Karma. Karma's assent was instantaneous. Of course, inside her machinery, algorithms computed his public standing, his request history, his intentions, and every other myriad variable against possible plotted outcomes, but that was the calculation of God, hidden in the tick of a second, and to Hamilcar, it seemed as if he were part of the whole glorious design, an extension of her will. It was difficult to remember that she had neither will nor desire.

"Let them in," Pande said to no one in particular.

"Watch them. Tally reports and give me highlights every three hours. And rate them for Human Intervention. They're prims. Might not understand how we work here."

"As you will, Sheriff," Karma said. Sometimes she had a damn strange sense of humor.

Chapter Four

King of Zeroes

The city was well ordered. Everything seemed restful, the leaves stirring with soothing breezes, the skies pristine, so the great mountains could be viewed from all angles. Gurung assured him that the air was full of microscopic nanotech, fighting the good fight, on spectrums far beyond human senses, and that Kathmandu was among the top ten cities in the world for safety. People walked the tree-lined boulevards with distracted eyes, reacting to invisible things, their lips moving, but everything was oddly silent, words carried away by some invisible wind.

"They speak with the Echo." Gurung tapped his head. "They see and hear and feel with it too. They do not see us."

Melek Ahmar felt the urge to roll a fist of air down the street, scattering these abstracted half men, upending them. He sent out tendrils of his disruption field, searching for any potency. Surely a place this grand would have hidden djinn in the center? Or had his people withered so far during his slumber? It did not bother Melek Ahmar overmuch. He held djinn and humans and all variations in between in equal contempt. He was singular. That's what it meant, to be *king*.

"There is nothing here to rival me," he said finally. "I sense no other elder djinn. The Marid will not come here, so far from the sea. Nothing can prevent me from taking this city."

They walked through the spotless, rolling streets, chased by a sweet-smelling breeze, the weather cool and pleasant enough to shed the bitter mountain chill from their bones, walking through the silent, busy people who seemed to dance to inaudible music. There was a peculiar tranquility to them, but perhaps it was just that their conflicts were hidden beneath the surface. Gurung led him to the foot of a grand spire, walled in, its true height lost in the clouds.

"My house was here," he said, tapping on the exterior gate. "Old family house. Little rickety place. This street was a dump before Karma came, full of hippies. Most of Thamel was like that."

"You are enormously wealthy then?" Melek asked. Hume wealth did not impress him much, but they seemed to set store by it.

"Not really," Gurung said. "Money's finished here. It's all Karma points, see? And when Karma requisitioned everything, it was like a slate being cleaned. Rich, poor, didn't matter. Usefulness. That was the key. Contribution to the system. You sell something you made, you get a fair price, Karma logs the value. Takes points from the buyer, gives 'em to you. You do some kind of public service, Karma gives you points. No more rich people sitting on their asses earning interest while we died in the mountains. We all thought it was a grand idea."

"Didn't work out, eh?" Melek Ahmar smiled. Backfiring wishes were a specialty of djinn, after all.

"Well, it did for everyone else," Gurung said. He flashed his insane grin. "Turns out I'm a zero."

"Zero. Yes, you probably are."

"Knife fighter, part-time chef, gambler," Gurung ticked off each thick finger. "Womanizer, if I do say so myself. Karma didn't rate me much."

"And where are all these other angry zeroes?" *An army of malcontents, waiting for me.*

"There weren't as many as you'd think," Gurung admitted.

"The God-Machine killed them? You alone escaped . . ." *Of course the tyrant would destroy his enemies immediately.*

"No, no, nothing like that," Gurung said. "She gave us all basic. That's the right to requisition basic shelter, food, drink, entertainment without any karma points at all. You could live and die, eat, sleep, fuck without a single karma point."

"So you get all that for free? And you're complaining? Sounds like a cut-price paradise. The gods promised far less, in my time." *And they delivered nothing, in the end.*

"Come," Gurung said. "Meet them and see for yourself."

They walked around some quiet streets that progressively got narrower, some of the marble cladding now turning to stone, then to brick, and while it was still pristine, there was a utilitarian cast to these structures. Even this sparkling city had an underbelly, it seemed, although to Melek Ahmar it reeked nothing of the desperation and fear that typically marked the Hume poor. They turned into a colorful street, festooned with ancient shop signs, proclaiming to be the infamous Freak Street, the heart of the old Thamel district. Of course, the shops were mostly shuttered now, and the drug-fueled hippies were long gone, but the ghost of their revelries remained, a peculiar haunting of good times past.

They stopped at a tavern, well lit, furnished in basic molded chairs, and an unmanned bar that seemed to be dispensing drinks using a system of hidden rails. Cubes of liquor shot across the bar and stopped in front of each patron. Other cubes flew in parabolic arcs across the room, landing on table tops with uncanny accuracy. At a human touch, the cubes unfurled into steaming containers, either chilled or hot. As the patrons drank, more and more of the container dissolved into the drinks themselves, until it was down to a shot carried in a paper-thin translucent glass, which disappeared into air within seconds of the last liquid drop being quaffed. Melek Ahmar, quickly used to the magic of the age, was unimpressed. Besides, he liked to slam his metal tankard on a table after a good drink. You could also brain someone in a bar fight, if you had a metal tankard. Couldn't brain a fly with these disappearing paper things.

He grabbed a flying cube from the air and drained it, waiting for some impudent fool to object. He loved bar fights. Nothing like stealing some fool's drink to get the juices going.

No one noticed. The thirty or so patrons carried on their conversations or eye blinking or whatever. The bar didn't even object; it just shot another identical container toward the waiting table. Melek Ahmar slumped. He had a feeling that it would continue doing so with infinite patience no matter how many drinks he kidnapped.

Gurung was well known here. He ambled from table to table with his bowlegged swagger, slapping people on the back, swooping down to kiss a couple of ladies on the cheek, and conversations started up; people jolted awake, remembering that he had no Echo, they broke out their dusty, unused voices, and he left a small trail of noise and laughter, of life, behind him.

"All zeroes here," Gurung said, settling down next to Melek after a few minutes. "There are bars like this throughout town. Zeroes tend to hang together."

Melek Ahmar looked around. They did not appear particularly discontented, this lot. He turned to the man next to him, a kindly older gent with neat clothes and a roguish air.

"So you lost everything to Karma, eh?" he asked. "Left to rot here in this bar, hmm?"

"Not at all," the old gent said. "I gladly gave it up. My name's Gaje. Karma came, what, twenty years ago? I had a shop selling fake Gurkha knives. The tourists used to lap that shit up. They'd buy two, three each, especially the young men. And I'd trot out that old canard, about how you had to blood the knife every time you took it out, like a true Gurkha. About half of those idiots would actually try to cut themselves. Of course, the knives were so dull they were never in much danger. Unless you count tetanus. Anyway, backbreaking, boring work for a pittance. I used to get up every morning and sit in that damn shop until ten at night. And then on the weekends I had to chase down all the drunken knife makers, like Gurung here, to collect my stock."

"Still, you were free as a bird before, right?"

"Not really. The air was so bad with nanotech and pollution that the birds all died. You couldn't see the mountains from here, can you believe it? We had to carry around portable nannite kits, just in case the air level hit red. Three times, I remember they issued citywide alerts, and whole neighborhoods had to go to slow-sleep until the nannite levels improved."

"Boring now, though, am I right? Nothing to do . . ." Melek Ahmar was getting irritated. These churls were all acting unreasonably cheerful for Humes. It was unnatural. What good were humans without their habitual dissatisfaction? It was their defining trait.

"Hah! I get up in the morning in my little place, and the kitchen unit makes a great roti breakfast. Better than my own mother's, believe it or not. I eat some yak cheese midday and then after a quick nap I hit the parks. I've got three girlfriends in three districts, do you know that? Gaje the Player they call me. Me, who didn't even have time to get married or have kids when I was young, thanks to the damn store. After I see to the ladies, I come here most evenings, for a drink and some backgammon, or ludo. We don't have anything to gamble with, true, since money was thrown out, but we put up little knickknacks, things of sentimental value. Makes the game spicier. And the best thing? No hangovers. I can drink as much as I like, and the little PMD just cleans it up when I sleep."

"You call this drinking?" Melek Ahmar looked around in contempt. No one was slumped over, no raised voices, no one was even laughing. And due to the stupid flying cubes there weren't even tavern wenches to molest. He thumped Gurung. "This is your bar of desperados? You want me to overthrow this God-Machine with these limp pricks?"

"They are a bit anemic," Gurung admitted.

"Overthrow Karma?" Gaje frowned. "I don't like the sound of that. I'm not going to report you, Gurung, because of that thing back in the day, but really, you ought to stop hanging out with degenerates."

"Degenerate?" Melek Ahmar grabbed the old man by the collar, shoved his teeth into his face. "I'm the djinn king Melek Ahmar, Lord of Tuesday, you old fuck! I can drink this entire city dry and still walk out. I'll fuck every man, woman, and goat in this miserable place and still be hard." He tossed Gaje into a table of aghast zeroes.

His distortion sphere flexed around him like a swarm of bees, a sound and atmospheric effect that made the Humes retch as he floated above them, his outline hazy with power, and landed with a crunch on the bar, cracking the hard laminate surface. His eyes were red, his skin red, like fire licking at the edges of it, and his archaic claims did not seem so funny anymore. The Humes cringed on the ground, expecting fury. But Melek Ahmar, at this moment, was not interested in destruction. He had been asleep for so long. What he really wanted was a good party. He grabbed the blinking bar unit and ripped it out of the wall. The drink cubes stopped their aerial ballet and fell helter-skelter, pelting the hapless customers. With two impossibly strong hands he wrenched off the bar counter itself, revealing a large stock of cubes underneath. If this was the only shit they had, this was what he would drink.

He started throwing them around. "Zeroes! Rejoice, for your king is here! Tonight we drink until the little machines in your spine cry for mercy! And enough of this blinking shit. Someone play some music!"

Zeroes stared at him, lost. Gurung got up from the floor, grabbed two cubes, and calmly drained them both. He grabbed two more, *bit* them in half, raw liquor sloshing over his face, tipped his head back, and gave out an ululating Gurkha warrior scream. Someone smashed a cube into Gaje's face, and the old man suddenly echoed Gurung's war cry, eating the cube like a watermelon, even as it dissolved into dark rum. The bar seemed to unfurl en masse, a bud suddenly flowering into something jagged and colorful. A couple jumped onto their table and began kissing, a group started singing loudly, off key and tuneless, but an old melody everyone knew. Zeroes around the room started leaping about, dancing, shouting; the party had begun.

Chapter Five

Sheriff John Brown

Hamilcar Pande lived in a modest ovoid building, far removed from the fashionable towers where the Kathmandu jet set played. He could have afforded more, of course: as a stalwart of Central Admin he had the points to requisition almost any living quarter. He was borderline ascetic, however, and all the indulgences of drugs and sex and Virtuality had limited appeal for him. There were people who staggered from orgy to mind-altering orgy, while their PMDs burned hot cleaning their blood, and it seemed to Hamilcar that they soon descended into one gigantic mindless beast, no longer harboring even the individuality they desperately craved.

He maintained real, if limited, relationships. He saw his parents once a month, at their home (they were still married) for dinner, which his mother still tried to hand cook, although that was nigh impossible now that all the ingredients came in cube form and were inevitably made of some variety of seaweed. Still, there were traditions to maintain, momos to pinch shut and steam, tea that had to be served a certain way.

His siblings lived all over town, and cousins and half cousins, and he conscientiously messaged them and attended reunions. They even had a family militant order of knights in Final Fantasy 9000, and played missions once or twice a month. He had no wife, but there was an attractive colonel who lived above him whom he had feelings for. Kanelia Shakia worked at Defense, which fielded a reserve force of human officers and soldiers in case the drone system ever went down. They mostly wargamed simulations and did live drills with archaic equipment. Karma kept human contingencies for everything, anticipating her own failure: necessary redundancies or busywork, no one was ever quite sure. Still, public service awarded points, and that was good enough for most people.

Once a week, Tuesdays in fact, Hamilcar had dinner with Colonel Shakia and then spent the night in her bed, where they had wild and inventive sex until exhaustion. He wanted more, but she had him on a strict schedule and seemed unwilling to deviate. He often wondered whether she had other lovers on rotation, but there was nothing furtive about the colonel, and he had never seen anyone else even visiting her, let alone spending the night. It was perfectly acceptable to have multiple partners, but Hamilcar was old-fashioned, and somehow over the past two years of seeing her, he had become half-enamored with her rigid routines.

This morning he woke up to find her gone, but she had made hot tea for him and left a sweet note. He was perfectly welcome to take his time, but alone in her apartment, he always felt like an interloper. The urge to root through her drawers or the back of her closet was almost irresistible, but Hamilcar was a man of honor. Besides, any illicit information would cheapen the hard-won confidences the colonel dropped to him from time to time, slivers of her life that he cherished and kept like polished stones in the back of his mind.

Her tea was excellent, made with perfect amounts of sugar and milk, stewed together in a pot rather than from the kitchen unit, so he drank it by the window, naked, and reflected on the city. He thought that perhaps he was a boring man, with a boring job, that somehow life kept him at arm's length at all times, as if he were merely gliding along the surface of the thing without ever experiencing the real blood and guts of it. Was this what the colonel saw in him, a prop, a mannequin man?

Was there anything such as achievement left anymore, anywhere in the world? There were still places hideously poor, places destroyed by nanotech, this was a planet of heaven and hell juxtaposed, post-human and stone age jumbled up, and he supposed he should be grateful to be living in the former. He *was* grateful. He believed in Karma with a confidence that far outstripped his belief in gods or nirvana. After all, he could see up close her workings. There was nothing secret about her algorithms; normal human minds couldn't follow them, but they could see the symbols and numbers whenever they wanted, study the bits that interested them. Which god had ever lifted her shirt and let the faithful look inside her skin?

When his tea was finished he washed the cup and pot and set them to dry. Then he dressed, made the bed, and changed her sheets and pillowcases, spending a last few minutes erasing any further signs of his ingress. He did this every time, although she never asked for it, never even seemed to notice it. This routine of physical work helped to center him, and seemed the least he could do, for messing up her orderliness. He took the stairs down to his own place, a bit heavyhearted as he was every Wednesday morning. Later, showered and shaved, he settled into his couch for some work.

Security reports were normal, point scammers, glitch riders, grifters were all within known parameters, the violent watch list was under drone surveillance, there was an uptick of noncitizens, but that was expected during this tourist season, and anyway, well-heeled travelers never caused trouble. The days of European backpackers looking for prayer wheel philosophy and life affirmation plus some cheap hash were long, long gone. Karma taxed visitors in hard currency, and they paid well to come see the Jewel of the Himalayas.

Something was bothering him, some tick under his skin, and it was well past lunch when he remembered the two rustics. No Echo, no PMD. He had requisitioned direct surveillance. Where was the report? He queried Karma and found a glitch. Not a glitch. More like an absence. There were a few images. Blurry. And then nothing. Large patches of time, nothing, as if the drones suddenly couldn't see in every frequency of light and sonar and magnetic fields. Drone failure was technically possible. Unlikely, but possible. So why did he feel a gut certainty that the rustics were responsible?

He blew up the pictures. Rustic One was big, hazy, of indiscernible ethnicity. He was the one wearing a goat. Rustic Two was unmistakably Gurkha. There was a look to his face, the deadpan expression, something pent up. What was it? Who was this man? He was not that old, why did he not have a PMD or Echo?

"Facial history search," he called to Karma. "Central Admin requisition account, please."

It was still official business. Hamilcar was scrupulous with requisitions. If it ever even *felt* personal, he would spend his own points, and let Karma decide on reimbursement.

"No citizenry of Kathmandu or any known incorporation," Karma reported. *So he doesn't belong to a foreign power, either.*

"Search pre-citizenry please. He's definitely Gurkha, so regional search. Requisition external records if required."

"External" were pre-Karma databases, which had to be paid for with hard currency from entities that were not on the Karmic points system. Hamilcar was actually affecting Kathmandu's external balance of payments from his couch, albeit in a miniscule way. Karma was following directions for now, like a normal input-output AI. If his query ever got more serious, she would take over, engaging higher mind tiers, and her analysis would reach levels far beyond human logic or serendipity.

This search took longer, long enough for him to have an illicit hand-rolled cigarette, the effects of which his body purged almost before the flame was out.

"Bhan Gurung. Eighty percent match."

"Good enough. Who or what is Bhan Gurung?"

"Male, early sixties. No permanent address, affiliation, or data trace. Recidivist, most likely."

"No scores? Not even guest scores?" Karma kept unofficial point scores for visitors, in case they ever wanted to requisition something against any good deeds. It was also a fad for travelers, to come to Kathmandu and accrue some of those famous karma points. She even issued certificates upon leaving, if someone had done something particularly useful.

"None. Not even any gaming records."

"So a luddite of some sort." A flash of insight. "Where was he, Karma Day One?"

A longish pause. He felt a flutter in Karma, as if a second gear of her mind was now engaging. "Prison. Death sentence. He was to be executed on Karma Day One."

"And you stopped it?"

"Day One was general amnesty, erasure of debt, cancellation of all contracts, deposit of all currencies, and nationalization of all private property," Karma said. "Yes, his execution was stopped with two hours to spare."

"What was his crime?"

"Records sealed and unavailable."

"He's *inside* our walls. Requisition in the name of national security!"

"Not sealed in an ethical sense. Hard sealed with crypto, and even then the files appear empty. Flushed. Records are physically unavailable."

"Even for you? I mean the top tiers of you?"

"There is no cure for full and final erasure."

"Is that even possible?"

"It is irregular. Many things were irregular before KD1."

"Can we pull him in?" Hamilcar asked.

"He has done nothing wrong so far. Pulling him in is not a requisitionable option at this point."

"Please run your advanced predictive algorithm for future threat levels."

"This is a problem," Karma said.

"What? Why?"

"The predictive algorithm is not working for them. The nameless male . . . Rustic One. He is blocking the algorithm."

"What? How? Is he a hacker? He's wearing a goatskin, for fuck's sake."

"Not hacking. By existing. He is blocking the algorithm just by being there," Karma said. There was a weight to her voice, as if an unknown number of mind tiers had crashed the conversation. "*Sheriff.* You are authorized to investigate in person."

Somehow the sobriquet did not sound so mocking this time.

Chapter Six

Goat Blood Café

Hamilcar Pande's first instinct was to confront the rustics. He was a straightforward man, unused to subtlety. By the time he reached their last known location, however, all he found was a quartet of distraught police drones and a completely wrecked tavern. He had seen some wild parties, especially in the tourist quarter, but this was insane. Every autonomous system had been dismantled, in most cases literally ripped out of the walls. Vomit, piss, blood, and unlikely amounts of semen pooled on almost every level surface, accompanied by lewd graffiti and knife marks gouging the walls, as well as various fist-sized holes, burns, acid scars, and other inexplicable damage, as if a convention of well-armed psychopaths had decided to distill their annual rampage into a single night.

Hamilcar was appalled. This was a zero bar, so technically there was no theft, as the drinks were free. Wanton destruction of property called for a negative balance, a karmic demerit, but in most cases Karma forgave minor debts. Here it was impossible to even levy it, for it seemed that whatever distorting effect emanated from Rustic One, it covered a wide enough area to obscure all the other patrons. The drone feeds had nothing but blurry faces, if that. For a system used to total and instant visual surveillance, this was disturbing. He could feel Karma's disquiet, and it upset him further.

"Shall I ferret them out?" he asked subvocally. "Surely there is enough cause now to eject them from the city."

"I cannot assess their threat level. Drunken debauchery is not sufficient cause for any action. I am curious," Karma said. "They appear harmless, yet this ability to avoid surveillance is disturbing. There might come a time when more overt threats utilize this camouflage. We require more information."

"Can you locate them?"

"Not precisely," Karma admitted. "By process of elimination, I can give you a probable area, perhaps a block. I think they are stationary somewhere. It is easier to find them if they move around. By my calculation of the depleted stock in this bar, the patrons present must have ingested alcohol and narcotic substances meant to supply two hundred people, yet there were hardly thirty individuals in here, including the rustics. They must all be comatose."

Hamilcar followed the trail of destruction to the back corner. Was that a decapitated goat? Ritually sacrificed? It was. *These people were disgusting. Where the fuck did they get a live goat?*

"I will investigate another way, then," he said to Karma.

Later, curled up in his couch, Hamilcar delved into the past. Karma Day One. The big change. It hadn't come as a surprise, of course. Months of debates, votes, warnings, fights. The consensus in the end had been either to try this radical gamble or to abandon the city altogether. The confluence of pollution, harmful nanotech, economic meltdown, and an angry, bitter population had made the leap of faith possible. So many people must have gambled on this day, anticipated the new world and how to get on top of it. Karma took everything; money, land, companies, stocks, bonds, vehicles, food, even a grandmother's famous momo recipe. It gave only one thing back. Points. Points for service, points for good works, points for intellectual copyright, points awarded by algorithms that snaked into the future, mathematical prescience that would have beggared the Oracle of Delphi.

Fair trade and good works, this was the basic heart of the system; Karma couldn't be swindled, she couldn't be bluffed, she didn't permit price gouging or fixing or hoarding or adulteration or IP theft, or all the unfair practices corporations used to control the economy, and despite the serpentine mathematics involved, the end result was simple—Karma made the market for every human transaction, big or small, and in circumstances of the public good, she awarded points herself. Altruism was a big thing these days, with god watching.

But just one time, on Day One, Karma gave points as compensation, for all the private property the city needed, all the things it deemed useful and "confiscated." Not money. Electronic money was deemed useless, artificial, fiat currency backed by nothing. Karma took physical infrastructure, physical properties, food stocks, and she put her own value on things, and this value was indisputable. There were no courts, after all, no appeals, only the tiers of her vast mind.

So some people had lost. The wrong kind of wealthy, the ones who didn't see it coming. But the clever ones *did* see it coming. They had done the math, had retooled their investments. There were men and women in this city with stratospheric karma, people who could requisition and repurpose entire city blocks for their personal use. Even in paradise, there were movers and shakers, people who could translate karmic clout into external force, whose tentacles no doubt extended to other cities. He glanced through the leader boards. Barsha. Doge.

Ankhit. Thapas. Basnyats. A few Pandes. Some old names cropping up, and some new.

So who was Bhan Gurung, to warrant a death penalty? And who was it that had the clout to destroy the records of his case? Someone who did it before Day One, who knew what was coming. Karma relied on databases. She needed information; without it she was blind. Almost forty years. Hamilcar smiled to himself. There were databases that could not be erased so easily. Data imprinted in meat. There were still people who remembered things from back then, who droned on and on about the good old days. He had to find that oft-ignored resource: old people.

A quick series of calls later, he found himself none the wiser. None of his thirty-six relatives over the age of fifty-five remembered any such case, no grisly murders, no sensational case, no Bhan Gurung. Many of them openly mocked him for being delusional. He expanded his conversations to general acquaintances, and still found nothing. Plenty of people seemed to remember the name Gurung, but whether this was the same man was highly debatable. One old gossip hound recalled a famous knife fighter from back in the day called Bhan Gurung, who most likely came to a disreputable end, for they always do, don't they? Another lady recalled having an affair with a dashing Gurung fellow who could snake up balconies like a flying eel, and oooh, imagine what he could do with those hips in bed . . . Of actual murder trials there was no recollection, not even from two foul-mouthed cigar-smoking octogenarian lady journalists who claimed to know where every single body was buried.

Later at night, even though it was not a Tuesday, he called the colonel, sketching out the case, and she reluctantly came over to help him brainstorm.

"A trial that no one remembers. It's crazy. A death penalty, and no one recalls a thing. Not even my great-aunt the judge."

"It's easy," the colonel said after a few minutes of wrinkling her forehead and thinking ferociously.

"Er, what?"

"If it wasn't a public trial it could have been a military one."

"Of course!" He kissed her on the lips. She kept them firmly shut.

"I have an uncle," the colonel said. "He used to be military police back then. I'll ask him."

"Now, please?"

"Yes, fine."

"And would you like to stay over? I'll get dinner . . ."

"It's not Tuesday."

"True. However, you're already here and there isn't, you know, a fine-print agreement about Tuesdays . . ."

"I'm not . . ."

"We could keep working on the case," Hamilcar said. "I already asked Karma, she said I could deputize you."

The urge to do something interesting won out. "Fine. Why not?"

"Great." Hamilcar beamed. "This is real, I feel it, it's important. It's not just busywork."

~

The colonel's uncle did remember. He had been a freshly minted brigadier in the army back then, when the army still meant regiments and guns and tanks.

"Bhan Gurung," he said. "That name haunts me still. He was a soldier in my friend's regiment. Gurkha, you know, they were all in the army back then. Bhan Gurung. That man could use a kukri. Three times champion in close-quarter combat, before he was twenty. He was a star, a stone killer, and his ancestor was a legend from WW2, Bhanbhagta Gurung, so the boys were in awe of him, even his commanding officer. Anyway, something happened, one day he snapped, broke into the compound of a very rich man and killed everyone inside. Twelve bodyguards, either decapitated or stabbed to death. Two cooks, three maids, the housekeeper, two bearers, all dead. The compound was an abattoir. The owner's family was not home, fortunately, for I'm sure they were the target. His younger brother was, and he died a gruesome death. Bhan Gurung tied him up and cut off bits and pieces until he bled out. The businessman himself barely escaped with his life. He arrived home midway, and Gurung waded through his guards and driver, stabbed him in the neck. By this point Gurung himself had been shot multiple times. They collapsed on top of each other, both on death's door. Both survived. Of course, the police came and then the military police took over. The case was hushed up, and the trial was closed doors. Gurung admitted to murder, there was hardly any need of a trial. Me? I didn't attend, no. Only three or four officers, I think, and they've all passed away. I remember talking to one of them after, General Thapa, he was the ranking chap at the rally, get this, he said this was the first time he had cried in all his life, since he was a toddler. I pressed him for details, but he never gave me any, other than saying that to a man they all wept, and Gurung was sentenced to death, and he refused to appeal."

"They *cried*?"

"I don't know why, he would never discuss it. I don't know what happened afterward, either. I suppose Gurung was executed. Karma came and the world turned upside down, and everyone forgot about Bhan Gurung. The rich man's name? I can't quite recall . . . He wasn't famous or anything, just some wealthy businessman, I guess. Dorji? Doje! That's it, Doje! It wasn't in the papers, Doje and the military hushed everything up. He wanted privacy, I guess, to protect his family. Hmm that's all? What a memory to bring back . . ."

Doje!

"He's number five on the karma scale. Doje. Has to be the same guy!" Hamilcar stabbed the list with his virtual finger.

"Fifth richest man in the city," Colonel Shakia said. She scanned his points history. "Exemplary life. Requisitions are nothing extravagant, not for someone his level. A lot of philanthropic work. Hasn't put a foot wrong since KD1."

"Why's he so rich?" Hamilcar asked. "Why does Bhan Gurung cause a small massacre trying to kill him? And why does he—or his people—erase all records of this crime?"

"I can answer the first one," the colonel said. "He got his points on Day One. Karma requisitioned all his property, and he had the buildings most desirable for her infrastructure. Not the most expensive land, mind you, just the most *useful*. Almost like he knew . . . So many points. Just for land? Something feels off to me."

"You ever wonder how it happened?" Hamilcar asked idly. "I mean how Karma came here?"

The colonel shrugged. "It was detailed in the KD1 announcement."

"Blah blah yes, the city was failing, we were losing the nannite war, there wasn't enough food or power or anything, people were literally about to eat each other . . ." Hamilcar said. "I'm talking about the actual nuts and bolts transfer of power to Karma."

"We had a plebiscite."

"Yes. But who actually brought the initial offer? Karma didn't appear out of thin air, where was she made? Who made her, and why did they pick us? Who negotiated on our behalf?"

"The government? What was it then, a parliament?"

"There barely was a government back then," Hamilcar said. "The city was failing, remember? No. I get the feeling Karma first approached the actually powerful people, the oligarchs, the nobles, the rich. People like Doje, maybe. And they negotiated in a way that let them preserve their clout. Look at the points list. Most of them made the top hundred on KD1, and have never left."

"But the system works," the colonel said with a shrug. "Who cares about the points? Karma saved the city, and now it's a wonder of the world. People thrive. There are no poor, no unhappy people. And Karma is merciful. She pardoned even Bhan Gurung, who murdered twenty-three people and crippled several more."

"Yes, I have not seen Karma falter at all. But this is *before* KD1. This thing happened when it was men in charge, and then the records were deliberately destroyed. So what I want to know is, why did Bhan Gurung kill twenty-three men and women to get to Doje?"

"That's a damn good question," said the colonel.

Chapter Seven

Djinn Kids Are the Worst

Melek Ahmar woke up feeling like death, his field fritzing like a knockoff two-bitto solar panel. Upon consideration, he had to admit this wasn't the worst hangover he'd ever had. To be honest, it wasn't even the worst this week. This robot bar knew how to make good liquor. His army of zeroes had somehow dissipated over the night. It had gone swimmingly at first, with blood oaths and goat sacrifices, but somewhere in the process the revolution had gotten derailed into a drunken orgy, which got further derailed into Melek Ahmar enthusiastically nailing as many humans of either sex as possible. Extreme blue balls: it's what happens after thousands of years in a stone sarcophagus.

It had been a good party. Part of the advantage of those little spine thingies was that the Humes now healed really fast. He was pretty sure he would have inadvertently broken many of them otherwise. Unbreakable Humes. *Not sure that's a fucking good idea, actually.* He sat up and spotted Gurung sitting by the window, drinking hot tea. The man was smiling, but it didn't seem to reach his dead eyes. He did that a lot, this Hume; stare off into space smiling like a kindly uncle, with those murder hole eyes. Melek ambled over.

"Good party. Those zeroes really got into it, eh?" he said. He stared at Gurung. The Gurkha did not appear the slightest bit wrecked. "You seem in good shape. Er, did you disappear sometime in the night?"

"Your plan of raising an army of malcontents is a failure," Gurung said.

"Yes, that's not my fault, your Humes here are completely spineless," Melek Ahmar said. "Why, they're not even into revolting! They seem to like this shit."

"Such is the problem. Zeroes will be zeroes." Gurung tapped a pattern on the windowsill with his ever-present kukri. "Are you still committed to ruling this city?"

"I am Melek Ahmar, one of the Seven Djinn Kings of the Earth," he said. The effect was spoiled a bit by the giant belch that escaped him. *What the hell did I eat? Or whom? Surely not one of the Humes?* "One city is not enough, but it is a start."

"Then we must change our tactics. Karma cannot be overthrown by force."

"I can level this city," Melek Ahmar said.

"Can you?" Gurung asked. There was a dreadful

hunger in him that set the djinn's skin crawling. Something was terribly wrong with his pet Hume.

"Well, hmm, not right now maybe. I mean, I've just drunk all night." Melek Ahmar flexed his field, found it still a bit fuzzy. He remembered it being a lot *harder*. Of course, the strength of the distortion worked with intent. You had to really want it. "But of course, if I kill all the Humes, then who am I supposed to rule over? Can't be a king without subjects. No point." *What's your grudge, eh, little Hume? Life seems perfectly bearable here. Why do you want to tear it down so badly?*

"You're a Great Lord of Djinndom?" Gurung asked.

"I keep telling you, I'm the Lord of Tuesday. You think they hand out days of the week just like that? I'm one of *seven*! And if the others are gone, as it seems like they are, for I cannot sense them, not even Horus the Broken, then I am now the foremost djinn walking this earth."

"There are djinn in this city," Gurung said. "Can you sense them?"

"Hmmph, if there are, they must be feeble things," Melek Ahmar said. *In truth I can't sense shit. Either my field is completely fucked or the djinn here are even worse off than me.*

"They say that there is a lady djinn who lives in the Garden of Dreams," Bhan Gurung said.

"Alright fine, let's go find this old hag." *Fuckity fuck. I*

*hate lady djinn. This dickhead is going to force me into some
quarrel and it's going to be Mohenjo Daro all over again.*

The Garden of Dreams was a marvel. It had always
been a place of serene, almost unearthly beauty, and
Karma had preserved it in spirit, while adding embell-
ishments from famed gardeners from all over the world.
Species of bird, fish, and squirrel lived here that were extinct in the outer world, a poignant reminder that the
Earth was not all paradise. This was wasted on Melek Ahmar, however, who cared nothing for plants or beauty.
Serenity wasn't his thing either.

This time of the day, the garden was somewhat empty,
though that still meant several hundred people sitting
around in contemplation. However, so cunningly were
the paths and grottos designed that each person felt enveloped in their own personal paradise, and hardly noticed the others. Melek Ahmar, of course, spoiled this by
stomping around and cursing when he got his feet wet in
the pond. He flared his power to steam them dry, which
scared the hell out of the fish and sent great ripples across
the pond, completely ruining the harmonic effect.

He felt an irritable ping across his field. Someone was
poking him! Melek Ahmar looked around, following a
buzzing noise that only he could hear, like a mild scratch-
ing on the corner of his eye. Gurung hurried after him,
tugging on his goatskin in concern. Melek Ahmar felt

the air change, as if he were walking through a membrane. Gurung yelped behind him, staggering back, and Melek Ahmar reached one hand behind and yanked his Hume through the barrier. They were now in a second garden, the real dream garden perhaps, one slightly crosswise and overlaid upon the earthly one, this one brightly colored and riotous, filled with ancient trees, where blue-tailed monkeys trolled the branches along with parrots, macaws, and feral jaguars, among other fantastic animals extinct or imaginary. Within it all, they could see the faint outlines of Humes walking around, insubstantial.

"What do you want?" an annoyed, girlish voice piped down.

Melek Ahmar looked up and saw a giant banyan tree holding up the sky, with a little platform on it, from which dangled a pair of muddy bare feet, attached to a small black-haired teenager smoking a lumpy hand-rolled cigarette on the verge of falling apart.

"Lady," Gurung said. He bowed deeply, and put a small offering of wild-grown tobacco at the root of the tree.

"My name is KPopRetroGirl," she said. "You know, 'cos I like that retro K-pop shit." She laughed at their puzzled faces and hummed a tune. "Just call me ReGi, okay?"

"I have no idea what that means," Melek Ahmar said. "I am Melek Ahmar, Mars, the Red King, the Lord of Tuesday, the Wrecker of Mohenjo Daro, the Most August, the Most Beauteous . . ."

"Yeah, yeah, I got it," ReGi said.

"You've heard of me, of course."

"Not really. You're the old guy that woke up. You upset the mountain goats."

"*Old guy?*" Melek Ahmar wasn't enjoying this at all. He hated djinn kids, they were the worst. Back in the old days they used to hunt down those snotty little bastards and stuff them in jars. *It's not like we need kids . . . we're practically immortal, for fuck's sake.* Which idiot had bred this little snot and then just left her here to annoy everyone?

"So anyway, what you want?"

"I want an army, little ReGi," Melek Ahmar said. "And you're the only djinn I've seen so far, so you can be my lieutenant. I'm going to take this city."

"Why?"

"Why? Because I'm the damn king of Mars! I'm supposed to bring war and pillage! And you're clearly my subordinate, my auctoritas is massively greater than yours, you look like you're an actual child, so you better do as I say."

"Or what?" She blew a smoke ring at him, and then blew another smoke ring *through* the original smoke ring. It was pretty cool.

Melek Ahmar was no braggart. Well, not entirely. When he flexed, he *flexed*. He sucked in his breath and jammed the distortion solid, expanding his quantum area effect to the max, like a peacock strutting his tail, except these were iron feathers slamming through the ethereal garden, flattening Gurung and the ReGi both, bending back those giant trees almost horizontal. He was so strong that even time stopped inside the pocket garden, bees caught in mid-flutter, buzzing in maddened panic, pollen dusting still life patterns in midair. Melek Ahmar held it an extra second for emphasis, and then sucked his breath back in, withdrawing the power, and the garden lived again, albeit in a state of disorder, as if a giant had kicked it sideways, which, on consideration, is exactly what had happened.

"You weren't fucking around," Gurung said, dusting himself off, "when you said you were the Lord of Tuesday."

Melek Ahmar bared his teeth. "Little ReGi. I can eat this precious garden whole. With you in it. I can hammer this precious little city so far into the ground it'll look like the head of a pin. Now get your ass off the ground and do as I say. Please."

ReGi picked twigs and leaves from her hair. Somehow she still had a lit cigarette, even though it was now bent forty-five degrees.

"Sir, yessir!" she said. She saluted and made it look entirely asinine. She then blew a final smoke ring for good measure.

Fucking djinn kids.

~

Request denied. Request denied. Twenty questions that came out the same way, despite Hamilcar using his maximum status, and the colonel going in with her official military requisition quota. Nothing. Sometimes he didn't understand Karma at all, had to remind himself that she was not a person as such, not a coherent mind, not one with intent, there was no conscious will in her cold algorithms, and this was what made her bearable after all, for people to be ruled by a system rather than a god. Still, sometimes, very rarely, the alignment of her equations were jarring, when it seemed her left hand was fighting her right.

Doje apparently spent a significant portion of his karmic points in maintaining privacy. And Karma, at least so far, was honoring it.

"No information, not even his birthday," the colonel said. "Do you realize, both Bhan Gurung and Doje are like ghosts."

"We know one thing. His address. He lives in the big tower."

"Great detective work. It's called Doje Tower, for god's sake. Good luck getting an appointment," the colonel said.

"No, but he's got to come out at some point," Hamilcar said. "And I happen to know that the best hole-in-the-wall momo place in town is just around the corner. You want to bet an old-timer like Doje is going to want hand-made momos? I've got an uncle who swears that the machine-made momos taste like shit because the pleats in the dough are too perfect, and you don't ever get the slightly burnt crunchy bits."

"People still eat food like that?" The colonel looked slightly grossed out.

"You've never been?"

"I like my food hygienic, thank you very much," she said. "And I don't want anyone's sweaty fingers near my momos."

"Hehe, I want to put my sweaty fingers on your momos . . ."

She gave him a blank look that was so daunting that Hamilcar cringed inside.

"So anyway, let's stake this place out. You can watch me eat, er, sweaty momos."

The colonel lasted half a day, driven off by the disgusting application of human fingers to dough and filling, the actual frying of dumplings in a wok full of hot oil. This was archaic stuff, a dying art, the smell of raw spices, the sizzle, the faint dusting of flour in the air. Hamilcar knew that the chef was not a zero, she had in fact a very healthy karmic balance, enough to requisition all of this raw material from Karma, ingredients that had to be fabricated from the city's own municipal microprinters, each strand knitted together molecule by molecule. Of course, there were more outlandish rumors that she also took raw food from the wild, stuff that actually grew on the ground; that thought made even Hamilcar squeamish.

In any case, the place was wildly successful, simply for the gimmicky variety of it, customers coming to see a pretty lady cooking and bantering all day from behind her glass barrier. Three days later, loitering in a momo shop with a bunch of zeroes, Hamilcar's gamble paid off. End of the third evening, during the busiest time, a pod pulled up, and a uniformed man swung open the door. Private security drones lined up discreetly. It wasn't loud or anything, that little thrust of privilege, but it was instantly visible to Hamilcar.

He slouched in the seat he had zealously guarded for the past seventy-two hours, and took a big gulp of beer to wash out his momo breath. Doje himself came out, a sleek white-haired man of indistinguishable age, a face that looked as if it had been ironed out, hair thick and perfectly coiffed, his posture upright and strong, despite what must be a hundred years of wear and tear. He exuded good health on an almost visible spectrum. Whatever PMD ran his body looked powerful enough to grow him an extra limb if he needed it.

He knew the chef, she called out to him, made him cut the line with good humor that negated any offense to the rest of the diners. "My old lover," she called him, making him blush and raising a cheer from the accumulated regulars, who had clearly seen this act before.

In this place, due to limited seating, there was a charming tradition of guests sharing the little circular tables, and also the first plate had to be eaten fresh off the oil or the steamer; takeaways were allowed, but discouraged, momos didn't keep well, after all, and as the place ran on the whims of the chef, her patrons always followed her little cues. Hamilcar, as it happened, had the only extra seat at the best table, the one that looked out into the whole room, while also giving a perfect view of the chef.

The bodyguard eyed him up and down, but Doje was a regular and shouldered his way through the crowd and took the empty seat, giving Hamilcar a friendly nod, barely waiting for his permission. Hamilcar let the man enjoy his first half dozen of the little steamed ones before breaking the silence.

"Doje. Number five, is it?"

The bodyguard, standing nearby, stiffened.

"Six," the man said after a second. "Although house rules are, no discussion of karma here. Everyone gets a momo, zero to one."

"Of course," Hamilcar said. "Forgive me. I was overcome with meeting such a man as yourself, at my humble table."

"Hmm. Karma is service, not rank. It is not a matter of pride to me, that I am six or sixty thousand or zero."

"An answer befitting your status, honored one," Hamilcar said. "Speaking of zeroes, I have recently met an interesting one. A man such as yourself, who has everything, will perhaps appreciate a good story more than anything else."

"You tire me with your obsequity," Doje said, bored. "Let me eat in peace."

"Of course," Hamilcar said coldly, with all the haughtiness of a man with generations of aristocrats lined up behind him. He had seen his grandfather adopt this very same posture countless times, and invariably resistance to his whims had crumbled in the face of sheer entitlement. Those days were long gone, of course, but humans still seemed to respond the same way.

"Oh, tell your damn story," Doje said.

"It's a story of a zero who miraculously escaped death years and years ago. No one knows why he was sentenced, why he was forgiven, or why he has returned here, but his name . . . his name is the stuff of legend: Bhan Gurung."

"Gurung!" Doje dropped his plate. "Who the hell are you?"

"Not Gurung, if you're worried," Hamilcar said.

"Gurung . . . He's dead in the mountains. He's a ghost. What do you know?"

"He's not dead, because I saw him last week," Hamilcar said.

"Impossible! I saw his PMD blink out on the machine. I saw his Echo fade away. You're fucking with me. He's dead."

"The man I saw does not have either PMD or Echo. He does not show up on surveillance. Karma cannot read him. It is possible to surgically remove your PMD and your Echo, given the will, the courage. Tell me, is the Gurung you know capable of such a thing?"

Doje shuddered. "Yes. Yes, it is possible, that psychotic man is capable of anything."

"Are you in fact the man he tried to kill, all those years ago?"

Doje stared at him. "You know I am, obviously. Now, Mr. Pande, what exactly are you after?"

"I work for Karma, Central Admin. I am an investigator," Hamilcar said. "*Sheriff*, she calls me sometimes. I understand this is some kind of ancient police rank, a joke of hers, I suppose."

"And what are you investigating, Sheriff?"

"Not you, sir," Hamilcar said. "Some weeks ago, Gurung and another man came into town. Neither have Echos or PMDs. We thought they were primitives who had somehow survived in the mountains. There are pockets of recidivists, even around here. I ordered surveillance drones. Imagine my surprise, then, to find that these men do not show up on any visual spectrum. Not clearly, sometimes not at all. I mention this detail only to impress upon you the difficulty Karma is in, her sudden uncertainty regarding the matter. If these men are here to harm you, sir, then I must be permitted to protect you."

"You?"

"I."

"I have guards. Drones."

"Your guards are hardly combat trained. And I have informed you that in our calculations, drones will not be effective. I speak for Karma. In this regard, I am given special emissary privileges. You may check."

Doje did just that, his eyes going blank for a second as his Echo went through the protocols. Then he grunted and looked at Hamilcar with renewed respect.

"Unlimited privilege, it says."

"I may pursue this case to the ends of the Earth," Hamilcar said. "Karma's estimations are that I am a frugal, conservative man, unlikely to abuse her power. In this, she is correct. I live for the job. I have determined that Bhan Gurung and this mysterious goatskin man want to kill you."

"You're a very blunt man for a government official."

"I am not a bureaucrat. I am the sheriff. Karma employs me for special cases only."

"And you want to save my life?"

"Assuredly. Allow me to join your entourage. Give me unfettered access, and I will try to capture these men."

"By using me as bait?"

"You are the target, I believe. I can spend all day trying to find these assassins, who are somehow avoiding karmic surveillance, or I can wait for them to come to me."

"And you are sure that these men are so very dangerous?"

"You have seen the license Karma has given me. Karma *herself* cannot predict what they will do ... Do you understand the gravity of that? Her predictive algorithms *do not work* on these men."

Doje shuddered. He had a distant look in his eyes, lost in the past, no doubt reliving the horror of that bloody day. "Yes," he said. "That is Bhan Gurung."

Chapter Eight

Old School

"We're in. He bought it. Gurung must have been one bad motherfucker. He's still scared of him."

"And me?"

"You're the muscle. Think you can handle it? There'll only be two of us."

"I can." There was absolutely no doubt in her.

The Doje Tower was self-named and rather ostentatious inside. Works of art, gilt ceilings, golden statues, looted temple doors, and priceless quantities of rare wood adorned every floor, getting progressively grander as they ascended toward the master's personal quarters at the very top. It was testimony to the sheer karmic balance of Doje, and to what extent Karma indulged her citizens. Curbing personal consumption had actually never been the point of her system, a thing misunderstood by many outsiders. In fact, with Karma and her ancillary automated systems doing all the heavy lifting, consumption was perhaps the main thing really left for ordinary humans to do. "Well, now you know what you get for that much karma," the colonel said.

Hamilcar ran his hand over a life-size golden Buddha. It might have been solid gold, for all he could tell. "The question is how he earned it in the first place."

"Do you think Gurung and the goat man will come here?"

"Without doubt," Hamilcar said.

"And how do we plan on dealing with them?"

Hamilcar pulled out a brace of weapons, old mechanical revolvers with long barrels. Karma had fabricated them at his request.

"One for you and one for me. The rustics can affect drones in some untested way, some kind of *interference field,* Karma says. Technological weapons might fail. They do not have PMDs, however."

"Which means gunshot wounds won't heal as fast as you make them," the colonel said. She was a weapons buff, knew her way around the revolver far better than Hamilcar. She had it loaded and cocked within seconds. "Clever." She took out a kukri, a well-serviced blade. "I've got a backup just in case. Mononuclear edge on this."

"Bhan Gurung was a knife fighter."

"Yes, that's why he probably won't be able to resist." The colonel re-sheathed her blade carefully. "It's coated with nerve toxins. Paralysis. And hallucinations. Apparently you see spiders burrowing into your skin for about six hours. Then you die."

Hamilcar stared at her.

"What? I got it from the archive of outmoded weapons. Sometimes old school is best school."

"After I'm done with Gurung, I might have to investigate *you*."

"Very funny."

"I'm not joking."

They found Doje eventually, at the very spire of his tower, meditating in an austere room, in stark contrast to the opulence below. It was windowed on all sides, stone floors and walls, and nothing much else, other than the thin mat the old man sat upon. The ceiling actually domed to a point on top, and was painted with religious symbols. Doje looked the colonel up and down, appreciative, acquisitive. Hamilcar saw her nostrils flare, and wondered if she would stab him with her poisoned kukri right then and there. He doubted he could stop her if she tried.

"So, this is the famed Kanelia Shakia."

"I am a colonel of the officers reserve. I prefer you call me by rank."

"Certainly, Colonel Shakia," Doje said with a bow. "I recognize you. Permit me to say that I greatly enjoyed your martial arts demonstrations. I particularly remember your MMA debut. A splendid rear naked choke."

Hamilcar raised an eyebrow. Martial arts? MMA? He hadn't ever searched her on the system, respecting her privacy. He was old-fashioned that way. She had never mentioned any professional fights.

"That was more than fifteen years ago," the colonel said.

Doje leered at her once again. "Yet I feel you haven't aged a day. I wonder how you would do against a professional."

"You have a professional handy?" the colonel asked idly. Her fingers were caressing the hilt of her knife in a way that boded ill for everyone involved.

"Look, Doje—" Hamilcar stepped up.

The colonel silenced him with a hand. She stood flexed on her toes, legs slightly apart, hands loose by her sides.

Doje snapped his fingers and a door slid open noiselessly. A giant neckless Mongolian gentleman came in with the serene gait of a mountain. His eyes swiveled between Hamilcar and Colonel Shakia, and he correctly identified her as the threat.

"A demonstration, please, Mr. Khunbish," Doje said.

Mr. Khunbish did not wait. He had a wrestler's stride, low and fast, bulling forward for a double leg takedown, knowing that once on top his weight would make him impossible to dislodge. The colonel met him with a knee to the face, which hardly slowed the Mongolian. She then sprawled forward around his neck, keeping her legs away from his grasping hands, and did some kind of swivel that had her on top of his back. Her right arm snaked under his chin and locked into her left bicep, her legs curled around his torso, and she hung on like a limpet mine as he struggled up with a roar. It seemed impossible, but Hamilcar watched in astonishment as the enormous Mongolian arced and shook and staggered, clawing back with his arms, trying everything to dislodge her. Frantic as the air began to leave his lungs, he started smashing his back against the wall using all his weight, trying to scrape or batter her off. Colonel Shakia just cranked her arm, her tendons jumping like cables, a bloody grin on her face.

Finally the Mongolian stopped his futile struggle. He gathered himself in, gritted his teeth, and clasped his hands together. Suddenly there was a muted crackle of electricity, popping noises, and the stench of charred flesh and smoke enveloped the fighters. Colonel Shakia let go with a startled yell, rolling back into a crouch, eyes narrowed and watering. Mr. Khunbish huddled where he stood, a shy smile on his face despite his obvious pain, his clothes hanging off in burnt strips, his spine smoking.

"An electric discharge, much like an eel," Doje said.

"To be used in desperation, of course. Still, I would call this a draw, no? Well done, Colonel Shakia. I feel impregnable in the protective circle of your arms . . ."

Kanelia Shakia was twitching from adrenaline and the electric shock. Hamilcar saw her hand moving almost involuntarily toward her gun, and he could picture a gaping large-caliber hole where Doje's forehead was, so he strode in front of her, lifted her up, and hugged her until her rage-filled shaking subsided, an infinitesimally brief second, before her eyes refocused into their customary coolness. Mr. Khunbish seemed to understand, cut from the same cloth perhaps, for he bowed slightly in apology, a traditional bao quan salute behind Doje's back, fist wrapped around his open palm, a gesture of respect between martial artists hidden from his employer.

"Thank you for the demonstration, Mr. Khunbish," Colonel Shakia said, returning his bow with a pranam, the Indian response. In this melting pot of Kathmandu, this city where the two great ancient cultures of the world collided, there were myriad gestures of respect, all understood in the minutiae of subtext. The pranam was also slight apology, for letting things get too far.

"Are you now convinced that between us we can protect you?" Hamilcar asked Doje.

The old man stared at him. "Protect me? Certainly. I have calculated Karma, Mr. Hamilcar Pande. What do you think the life of one Bhan Gurung is worth?"

"What?"

"What if Mr. Khunbish here were to rip his head from his body, a feat I am assured he is capable of with his bare hands? On my account, hmm? What karmic penalty would our beloved ruler levy on me?"

"You are proposing murder."

"You see, I think my account would be able to bear the cost. I have been saving up good deeds my whole life, eh? I think Karma would allow me to kill your Bhan Gurung in broad daylight without batting an eyelid. I think I could order his execution the minute he walks in this door and my credit would hardly suffer. In fact, I think I have such a head start that I could order *your* death, and that of the delectable colonel, and your boss would let me. Oh, I might feel the pinch, but you, with your precious carte blanche, *you'd be dead*. What do you think of that, mighty sheriff?" Doje's eyes flared out with madness.

"My poor children, you think anything has changed? You think your god of algorithms means you're safe from *me*? You think I do not have twenty Khunbishes? You think I cannot castrate you in front of your bitch and watch you bleed out without Karma twitching? So yes, certainly I feel protected. And Gurung will come to me, yes, and you will be duty bound to step in front of him, even if you loathe me. And if he gets past the good colonel, no doubt you will heroically sacrifice yourself. And when both of you are dead, Khunbish will fight. And when Khunbish dies, two more of his soul brothers will step up and then two more. And when the dead are piled high enough, finally I will be rid of this curse."

Chapter Nine

Papa Tuesday

"Pops. Pops. Papa Tuesday. Yo."

Papa Tuesday? Really? "What? What do you want?"

"Just sayin', Pops. What's the plan here? Gurung's spilling pistachio shells all over the garden, man. Can you tell him to stop?"

"Not Pops. No Pops. No Papa. Melek Ahmar. Melek Ahmar. The . . ."

"Yeah yeah yeah, the King of Mars, the Lord of War, I gotcha, Papa Tuesday."

Is there anything worse than a snarky djinn-girl teen? Is there? I don't think so.

"So Pops, word is, you're past it."

"What?"

"Past it. Heard you're washed up. Has been."

"Fuck off! I'm busy."

"Hey hey hey, don't shoot the messenger. What I heard. I didn't say it." Her outrage was over the top and absolutely real. Which meant, of course, she had totally said it. "They're saying all your buddies are gone and no one remembers you or gives a shit. About you."

"If, as you have repeatedly mentioned, Horus and Memmion and Kuriken and Davala and all the others are gone, then it merely reconfirms the fact that I am the most powerful djinn left in this world! There's no one alive who can match me. You are lucky you have—"

"Yeah yeah, I understand that, it's just that Hazard rules around here, and they're saying if we make too many waves he might come over and squash us." ReGi was relishing her role as chief tormentor and had taken to literally stalking Melek Ahmar around the off-kilter garden.

"Hazard?" This was a name new to him. "Who the fuck is that?"

"You know, deadly duelist, undefeated . . . ?"

"Duelist? I don't duel. I use my mace to flatten mountains."

"Yeah, and rivers and lakes and stuff."

"No . . . what? How can you flatten a lake?"

"Never mind. Hazard. You know, Hazard. Dark, sexy, and handsome? Mysterious air? Kind of brooding all the time?"

"I don't have a fucking clue who this Hazard is, but he's beginning to piss me off just for being a dickhead . . ."

"Come on, everyone's heard of Hazard . . . he's like a

rockstar," ReGi said. "All jackally and shit . . ."

"Wait. Jackally?"

"Yeah. Jackal head, duh."

"Jackal head. You couldn't have led with that?"

"So you *do* know him, huh?"

"If you're talking about Anubis, then yes, I know the kid. Can't be two assholes wearing jackal heads. I once stuffed his ass in an inverted underground pyramid. Took him twenty years to get loose. If that's the best you've got . . ."

"Your funeral," ReGi said sotto voice. "So Pops, like I'm totally stoked to join your three-man army and shit, but what the fuck are we actually doing?"

"Gurung is making a plan," Melek Ahmar said loftily.

"Gurung? Uncle Gurung?"

"Yes."

"The old dude who's *not* a djinn?"

"Right."

"Whose special power is eating pistachios?"

"Hrrrm, yes."

"So like he's the man with the plan?"

"Well, he's the native informant, right? Our inside man, isn't he? And you have to admit, he hates these bastards," Melek Ahmar said. "I mean, I just wanted to rule this place, but he's pushing for total destruction. Tear out every brick and sow salt in the earth type of thing. Wants to rip out Karma."

"Yeah, about that," ReGi said. "Don't you think that's a bit abnormal? Like I don't know about you, but I kind of like the city. Couldn't you rein him in a bit?"

Melek Ahmar looked gloomy. "Between you and me, he's a bit scary. I mean, not to me, of course, but I can see how he'd terrify the Humes. He's always smiling, right? But look at his eyes. Nothing."

"Yeah, he's a psycho, Pops."

"Shh shhh shusshhhh, he's going to hear us, he's coming . . ."

"Djinn." Gurung gave them a short bow.

"Hume," Melek Ahmar responded. The smiling Gurkha looked unusually grave.

"There are no rebels left in this city," Gurung said. "No army to raise, no gangs, no malcontents. Karma sees everything and she gives value to all."

"Oh well, too bad, then," Melek Ahmar said with a smirk. "No use kicking up a fuss. We'll just squat around here until someone kicks us out . . . Or tries to, anyway. The tourists from hell is what Karma's gonna get. What I want to do is get into some of those fancy bars uptown . . ."

"But you're a king!" Gurung said, a glint in his eye.

"Eh, yeah, but I'm on sabbatical . . ."

"We cannot brook this kind of dishonor."

"Look, I mean, I appreciate it, but really, no need to go out of your way . . ."

"There are other ways to skin a cat," Gurung said. "A king you are, noble lord of Tuesday, and a kingdom you shall have, this I have sworn, when you took me into your service."

"Eh? You did? I did? I mean, did I take you into service? I don't exactly recall . . ."

"I have sworn!"

"Ahem, yes, of course, if you've sworn." Melek Ahmar looked helplessly at ReGi for support, and only got a roll of her goth-black eyes. That was the problem with djinn. They never stepped up. "Irrevocable blood oath, was it?"

"Is there any other kind?"

"Of course not." *Bloody irrevocable blood oaths. Never take smiling Gurkhas into service while tipsy. This must be added to the Lore.*

"The points. Karma gives points according to calculations. She does not choose," Gurung said. "My King, if you had the most points, if you had enough points to beggar the entire list, you would rule *through* Karma."

"But we're zeroes," Melek Ahmar said. *Thank god. Being a zero looks pretty good about now.*

"The Lady of the Garden is not," Gurung pointed out.

"What? You've got points?" Melek Ahmar scowled at her. "How?"

ReGi shrugged. "I'm the djinn of the garden. People come here with all kinds of ridiculous wishes and stuff. Sometimes I help them out. Karma gives points for being helpful, you know, you should try it sometime."

"You're sitting here giving *wishes*?" Melek Ahmar bristled. "Like a fucking genie in a lamp?"

"Hrrmmm *drugs,*" Gurung coughed.

"What?"

"I believe the lady actually dispenses drugs."

"Yeah, so?" ReGi said. "Look, like Gurung says, Karma doesn't make value judgments. People want drugs sometimes that they can't get from the synthesizers, and I give them to them. Herbalists, you know, nature lovers. I'm actually keeping alive ancient traditions and culture."

"So Karma is giving you points for selling drugs to people?" Melek Ahmar asked. "This isn't illegal in any way?"

"That's what people still don't understand about her. Karma isn't aware. She doesn't have a moral precept. She ratifies the market whenever there's a free trade. She gives fair value to everything, by calculating to a preciseness that is humanly inconceivable. So no one gets cheated, everything is true value, but ultimately that value is determined by what people want. Provided you don't destroy city functions, you can do whatever you want under fair market value. Ergo, people give me points and I give them drugs, and because they're rare, Karma fixes a high value on the commodity."

"So for example, if everyone wanted Gurung dead, then I would get points for killing him?" Melek Ahmar asked.

"Well, I suppose, yes. Although presumably her predictive functions wouldn't let it get that far," ReGi said.

"Not that everyone wants you killed," Melek Ahmar said hastily to Gurung, who had begun to unconsciously fondle his damned kukri. "Figure of speech. So why hasn't this oracle-machine arrested us? Surely they must know we are here to conquer?"

"That's the beauty of it," ReGi said. "Our distortion fields cause interference. The predictive functions don't work with djinn, especially ones with very strong fields. Apparently the distortion sphere causes so much basic quantum uncertainty that mathematically it is debatable whether we even exist or not."

"Is that so? So the oracle is blind to us? Thus they cannot predict the societal harm you are doing with your petty drug business . . ."

"Herbal business!" ReGi snapped. "And I'm making everyone very happy, thank you, I'm one hundred percent organic. Try smoking that vat stuff and tell me I'm causing harm!"

"The lady is 478 on the list, I believe," Gurung said.

"You're in the top five hundred?" Melek Ahmar said. "From selling *weed*?"

"I've got a big garden." ReGi smirked. "One hundred percent organic leaf, baby. Priceless stuff."

"Right, I'm taking this venture over," Melek Ahmar said. "And we need to start selling harder stuff. It'll be a lot easier to get to the top from 478 than from zero."

"Precisely my thinking, Lord," Gurung said.

"Hey!" ReGi said.

"You want me to flatten everything for real?" Melek Ahmar asked.

"Fine. Just muscle in. See if I care."

"Look don't worry, when I'm king, you'll be my deputy king for sure," Melek Ahmar said. "I'll flatten that tower Gurung stares at all day and turn it into one giant garden for you."

"We will tear it down, yes," Gurung said with a smile. "But it will be a mausoleum, I think."

Chapter Ten

Garden of Ridiculous Demands

Melek Ahmar sat in a very uncomfortable chair. Gurung had procured it from somewhere. It had great arms and a sprawling ornate back and thick curling legs, a grotesque gilded runaway exercise in wood carving by some megalomaniac carpenter with delusions of grandeur. Throne. It was actually a throne. There were dragons and apes and rams carved into it. One of the ram horns was digging into his back. He had suggested they operate from the shadows like ReGi, but Gurung insisted they needed a spectacle.

"It'll bring the punters faster, he said," Melek Ahmar muttered. "I've got to look like a king, he said . . ."

The first ten customers, predictably, were there for ReGi's magic THC-aligned organic weed, which grew by the bushel in her alternate garden, and they were slightly nonplussed at his glorious majesty. Still, as his voice thundered out gibberish, making their bones quake, and oversized bags of weed appeared in their hands, they were reasonably pleased. A few judicious pricks from Gurung's kukri encouraged half-hearted bows and curtsies, until the rest of the line caught on; there was new management in town, and a bit of bowing and scraping was necessary.

The eleventh guy was different. He came in holding an urn and caused an immediate furor. Gurung, fielding the wish-makers in his laconic manner, looked up with a frown.

"He wants his wife's ashes scattered on the Kanchenjunga."

"Is she dead already? Or do we have to take care of that as well?"

Gurung gave him a weird look. "Yes, yes, she's passed already."

Melek Ahmar shrugged. Who knew, with Humes?

"Top of those mountains, right? So that's not hard, is it? Why can't he get up there?"

"It's forbidden to climb, first of all, and secondly, there's no microclime, he'd be dead half a day outside the city limits," Gurung said. He shrugged. "*You* could get up there, but it would take you weeks. Seems like a hassle."

"Weeks? That was when I was weak." Melek Ahmar smiled. "Watch, Hume, what a King of the Djinn can do."

He leapt off the chair, which had already murdered his spine, and sucked in a lungful of power. Ahhh. It felt good to flex everything. His distortion field thickened around him into a palpable black aura, and he could sense the Humes retching and writhing in its proximity, an unfortunate effect of the particle-twisting nature of distortion itself. He grabbed the hapless widower, tucked him under his arm, and launched himself into the air, a homing missile aimed at the clouds, his raw power streaking behind like the tail of a comet. Within seconds the city was dwindling beneath him, and the man under his arm was shrieking in fear. Ahhh. This was it. Air rushing at you, birds flapping away, a struggling Hume in his talons, what sport!

Melek Ahmar returned to the garden several hours later. He was slightly bedraggled, but that was to be expected, given he had been bouncing off mountains. A very large crowd had gathered, awaiting his return, the air abuzz with excitement and conjecture. People craned their necks to get a look at him, or the hapless widower. Who was unfortunately not present.

"We had a slight accident," Melek Ahmar said. "He wasn't enjoying the jumping around and flying."

"What? Did you leave him in Kanchenjunga?"

"Look, he said any mountain would do at that point, so we picked one of the closer ones."

"Showoff," ReGi said.

"So where is he?" Gurung asked.

"He died, just like that. His heart gave out." Melek Ahmar looked up with a kind of wonder in his eyes. "So fragile. He smiled at the sun. Said it was beautiful. Then he was gone. So I burned his corpse and scattered his ashes with his wife's."

"He *died*?" Gurung spat. "So. Negative karma."

"Hold on." ReGi was staring into space, her implants scrolling data across her eyes. "He died happy, you said?"

"What do I know?" Melek Ahmar groused. "I held his head up so he could get a good long look across the sky. Fucking Humes."

"Must have been a good fucking view, dude," ReGi said. "He gave you everything. Every single point with his last breath. It's a fair trade. Karma ratified it. He had no one else, no living family. You made his day, apparently."

"Fucking Humes," Melek Ahmar said. *They break so easily . . . why the hell aren't they more careful?*

Gurung beamed. His knife flashed in his hand as he cleared the gawkers. "Next!"

~

Hamilcar lay supine on Doje's couch as layers of data cascaded over him: grainy images, drone infrared and raw footage on spectrums only the Echo could decipher; garbled audio like the imaginary susurration from an ant farm; the click counter of karma changing fast, of the algorithm firing like an ancient stock market bull run; a sweaty, stocky beast of something snarling in the serene Garden of Dreams, a garden suddenly hazy and inaccessible to their mechanical eyes. He was covered in sweat. The data was relentless, frenzied. Tiers of Karma's mind were now focused on him with a palpable weight, a gravity that he had never experienced, as if he were strapped to a gigantic wheel whose inevitable turn would pulp him any moment.

Kanelia Shakia had her own feed, lay in her own pool of sweat, her weapons laid out in front of her like fetishes. Gurkha knife. Gun. A newly acquired electric wand, designed for stunning. Three metal pinballs, drones that could fire up into the air like attack hornets, controlled by Echo. Her lines of inquiry were military: defense of the tower, and a possible invasion of the garden. She was held in rapt attention, a child wandering through the deadly basement of Karma's arsenal, a shop seldom open for humans.

"He's granting wishes," Hamilcar said at last. "That's the only explanation. I don't know how."

Statistics slammed into his Echo, making him groan. Murders, up. Robberies, up. Assaults, up. Suicides, up. Destruction of property, up. Use of illegal and arcane weapons, up. Bizarre and unnatural sexual acts, up. Recidivism, up. Every bad metric up, as if some base craving for disorder and pent-up lawlessness had been unleashed in the populace. And on top of everything, a plethora of weird anomalies such as flying men and giant ghost trees, Kathmandu transplanted into the middle of a jungle, as if the garden existed in two forms overlaid upon one another, one tranquil and the other full of primordial beasts.

It all came from verbal accounts, fevered dreams of men and women, of the thousands who now thronged that damn garden, all they had to go on with the failure of electronic surveillance. Karma was flying in blind, and beginning to comprehend the dismaying fallibility of the human mind, running up against the wild drinking gleeful satyr of chaos loitering inside the hindbrain, demanding to call the shots.

"He is accruing karma points at an alarming rate," Karma said.

The Karma ticker momentarily overlaid Hamilcar's Echo and he almost yelped. "Shut it off! He's already in the top two hundred. Why are you *still* giving him points?"

"It is the algorithm," Karma said. "My job is not to assign value. I merely ensure a true fair market. Ultimately, the actual value of anything depends on you humans."

"But . . . but he's helping them *murder* each other. He's making them *deviant.*"

"I think they were already deviant," Colonel Shakia said with a tight grin. "They're all rounded up in one place. Why don't we just nuke the damn garden and get it over with?"

"What? Are you crazy?" Hamilcar trailed off as he saw Karma actually computing the cost benefit of this proposal.

"Is that your formal suggestion, as the lead Defense member of this committee?" Karma asked on the audible channel.

"Committee? What the fuck? Now we're a formal committee?" Hamilcar asked. Both women ignored him.

"It is," Colonel Shakia said.

Karma whirred some more. "Regretfully the loss of life and general uncertainty of the outcome renders this option currently negative in value."

"Uncertainty of outcome?" Colonel Shakia raised an eyebrow.

"The effect of our fusion weaponry on Rustic One, Lady ReGi, and the garden itself is uncertain."

"You're telling me *a nuke* is not certain to kill them?"

"Correct."

"Hmmm." She unconsciously fondled the butt of her gun.

"Tell me you're not seriously considering blowing up the city," Hamilcar said.

Colonel Shakia shrugged. "I'm the military option. That's my job. You're the investigator. You find a different solution, if there is one."

"Or else?"

"Eventually we—I—will go in with an extraction team and find out the hard way."

"Karma, I think we can all agree we are dealing with nonstandard humans here?" Hamilcar said.

"Almost certainly."

"Alien? Something technologically augmented? Some kind of post-human?" He asked.

"Djinn. At least Rustic One and Lady ReGi."

"I see." Hamilcar did not see, but if Karma believed in djinn, who was he to argue? "Look, Rustic Two, Gurung, he's the interesting one. Don't you get it? What's he doing there among these . . . these djinn? He's the one who knows the city, he's the one with some axe to grind."

"So?" Colonel Shakia asked.

"So he's calling the shots. I don't know how, but he's the one making their agenda. He tried to kill Doje before, and possibly he wants to kill him now. The real question is why. What the hell happened back then?"

Hamilcar could almost taste the reluctance of Karma to answer.

"Information immediately prior to KD1 in this issue is not accessible."

"To us, or to you?" Colonel Shakia asked, suddenly paying attention.

Excellent question, Hamilcar thought. *You are an investigator after all, my dear colonel.*

Karma was silent. It was unnerving. He could not tell if she was unwilling or *unable* to answer.

"Let me ask a different question," Hamilcar said. "We found out that Doje purchased many private and public properties, prior to KD1, which were subsequently requisitioned by the city. That's how he accrued so much karma. I found certain old newspaper records, which reported an approximation of Doje's wealth prior to KD1, among other members of the plutocracy. Converting the entirety of his value to bitto, and taking into account property prices of that era, there seems to be a gap. He was not among the city's wealthiest men, certainly not from the noble class, yet he was able to fund huge cash purchases on the eve of the plebiscite. Where, dear Karma, did he get his funds?"

"It is not pertinent to this investigation. Doje is not under investigation."

"I see," Hamilcar said. *It fucking is pertinent.*

"Find another way, *Sheriff,*" Karma said. "Negotiate

their exit from this city. Or Colonel Shakia shall lead the strike team in."

Colonel Shakia got up from her couch and stretched. Her face was, as ever, inscrutable. "I'll get cracking on that, then."

Chapter Eleven

Suitors

Melek Ahmar sat on the ledge of the great tree house, dangling his feet, savoring the cold and the darkness. There was a slump to his back, a disaffection to the way he was puffing on his cigar, normally one of the highlights of his nightly ritual. He heard the clumping noises of ReGi's footsteps, those disgusting clog-like boots she wore, god knows how she kept on her feet let alone skittered along the branches as she did, that damn girl was half chipmunk, he really ought to get to grips with her lineage, but damned if he had the time . . .

She settled down beside him, their distortion fields powered down, but still causing a spark or two as errant molecules collided. There was a reason most djinn stayed well away from others of their kind. He looked at her profile and sighed. When she didn't respond he sighed again, this time with so much gusto that the cherry fell off his cigar and he had to light it all over again, which he did with one fiery forefinger.

"What is it?" ReGi finally asked with a smirk.

"Just did in a grandmother. Gust of wind. Blew her right out of her window. Third one this week, can you believe it?"

"Humes," ReGi said. "The shit they wish for . . ."

"I can't understand it," Melek said. "Everyone keeps wishing for death and destruction. Other day, one woman wanted an earthquake. Just a small one, so her in-laws' house would fall into the abyss. Great plan, except she was living next door. So of course half her place fell in as well. No one ever wishes for anything good . . ."

"I guess Karma gives them all the good stuff," ReGi said. "You're kind of the antithesis. Melek Ahmar, the darkness in their souls, made incarnate."

"It's Gurung," Melek Ahmar snuffled. "He's the one screening the petitioners. He keeps picking the worst ones, I know it. He hates everyone here. He's enjoying it, every time they want something terrible. It's the same old story. He picks fights all day and it's poor old Melek Ahmar who has to do the smiting. No one ever thinks of me. Did he ask me if I wanted to off old ladies and turn wine sour? Did he ever ask me if I wanted to sit on that horrible throne and listen to every disgusting gripe from miserable Humes all day? No. He did not. Motherfucking Gurung. He's not going to be happy until everyone wishes everyone dead. I just know it. And then he's going to make me kill them turn by turn."

"Poor old Pops," ReGi said. "I thought this was your oeuvre, you elder djinn granting wishes in a fucked-up way . . ."

"Yeah, that's like when someone asks for a bucket of gold and you put the bucket down a well full of poisoned snakes, and laugh at him while he gets bit," Melek Ahmar said. "That's time-honored fun. That's in the Lore. This shit? This is just dark. These Humes are crazy. What happened to asking for money and houses and young lovers? What happened to asking for a bigger dick or bigger tits, eh?"

ReGi laughed. "They got that shit already, Pops, don't you see? They just need you for the bad stuff. Funny thing is, after this is all over, I bet they'll all say *you* made them do it."

"Fucking Humes," Melek Ahmar sighed. "All I wanted was a good party."

~

Hamilcar went back to the brigadier, this time in person, alone. The urge to walk the streets, hands huddled in his coat pockets, was strange to him; even stranger, putting his Echo to sleep so that his eyes actually reverted to their natural state, a view curiously empty of input. It was a subconscious act, a rebellion unthinkable even three days ago; a physical meeting, Echos off, out of surveillance, a conversation with a low chance of being picked up by Karma, unless she had drones on him, which was possible, of course, but unavoidable. Had he vocalized his intentions, it would have shaken him to his core; he was looking to subvert the state. He wanted secrets the God-Machine was unwilling to give.

Brigadier Uncle was just as shocked to see him in person, but old habits kicked in and soon they were sitting in a square balcony full of potted plants, having a nice cup of tea. Aunty Brigadier provided a platter of biscuits and cake, asked him a few pointed questions, and then left them to their "man talk" with a last forbidding glare. Exactly what perversions she expected him to lead her husband into in full sight of the street was a mystery.

"So, young man, you're the one stepping out with our Kanelia, eh?" the brigadier said after an uncomfortable silence. "Ahem. I hope I'm not being old-fashioned, but are you from the Ganesh Pande line, or the railroad Pandes?"

Of course. They think I'm here to propose.

Hamilcar, unsure how to stop this elderly barrage of polite inquiry, soon found himself delving exhaustively into the bones of his family tree, elucidating in depth every connection and childhood memory he could dredge up. They moved on to his elementary school grades, his sporting achievements, his choice in haircuts as a young man, and some comically ham-handed detective work into his alcohol and drug habits. Since the colonel could easily drink him under the table, he bore all of this with good humor and won the brigadier over. It was quite some time before he even remembered that he was not, in fact, here to get married.

"And, of course, you'll get out of those dreadful government quarters, eh?" Brigadier Uncle said with a chuckle. "Need a bigger place, hmm? I'm sure you'll want to have some kiddies . . ."

"Right, right, sir, actually, I'm sure you know your niece very well."

"Of course, of course."

"Then I'm sure you'll understand that all decisions about everything will undoubtedly have to be made in consultation with her, including marriage."

"What are you saying?"

"I'm saying that I'm not at all sure she'd say yes to marriage, let alone children."

"What? But haven't you even asked her yet, you daft boy?"

"Ah no, I have not."

The brigadier looked dismayed. "What the devil are you doing here, then?"

"I wanted to chat about that case of ours."

"The old Gurung one?"

"That's right."

"And not about getting married?"

"Not right now, no sir."

"But damnation, man, you can't carry on this way . . . surely you mean to get married at some point? You're the first man she's ever introduced to us . . ." He looked ready to cry.

Hamilcar leaned back in his chair and seriously considered this question. Of course, they had never spoken about the future, she barely acknowledged any plans beyond the immediate week. He didn't even know her views on marriage or children; these things had never come up. On the other hand, he couldn't quite imagine life without her glowering in close proximity.

"Honestly, I wouldn't mind," Hamilcar said. "I mean, I love her, I guess."

"Have you told her this?"

"Do you not know her at all? She's not a feelings sort of person. We don't have that kind of conversation."

"Well, woo her properly, for karma's sake!" The brigadier lit up an illicit pipe and indicated that this was going to turn into a reminisce of days gone by. "Do you think your Aunty Brigadier just fell into my lap, a woman like that?"

"She must have been a rare catch," Hamilcar said.

"Twenty suitors, each one richer than the next!" the brigadier said. "She was like Helen of Troy. Every morning the street under her balcony would be strewn with flowers. I wrote thirty-two poems to her, each one a masterpiece. When I got shot, dead on the cot in the middle of nowhere, she finally replied. One word: 'Yes.' A lady of brevity! Alas, if only that were true now. No, but that's what it took to convince her."

"You got shot?" Hamilcar asked.

"Training accident," the brigadier said hurriedly. "Gun went off by mistake. Ahem, that's not the point. Thing is, you've got to make it happen. Do something. Don't just sit around."

"Yes, sir."

"In that case, boy, let me be the first to welcome you into our family."

"Let's not jump the gun, Uncle, I don't think the colonel, er, Kanelia, has any idea about this. Why don't you wait for my signal before telling everyone . . ."

"Quite right." The brigadier winked at him.

"So about the other matter."

"Gurung?"

"Doje. The businessman who was attacked."

"The victim?"

"Yes, well, I'm wondering about that. Was he a famous

man, do you remember?"

"Nothing really, I knew he was rich, not sure what he did. As I recall, details of the case were not published."

"As far as I can tell, he came into a lot of cash right before KD1. Money he used to purchase properties which in turn were converted into karma. Five, ten million bitto maybe. How would one get that much money back then?"

The brigadier snorted. "You youngsters don't even know anything about money. Money used to make the world go around. People would sell their mothers for money. Things were bad back then, everything was collapsing. Whole communities were disappearing. Do you know how quick people can die in a bad swarm of nanotech? Minutes. Skin shredding in front of your eyes, bodies just melting. We couldn't make the good stuff fast enough in our bodies then, not with the old PMDs . . . Cities, towns, everything was on a knife's edge, even with AI running the systems. Too many people, you couldn't give them food or water. Too few, and you couldn't make a viable microclimate with the nanotech. It was all guesswork, even AI couldn't calculate it all fast enough, and people just died. I've seen highways full of the dead, people dropped where they stood. You kids live in paradise now, you don't even know it."

"Can you think of any city financial records anywhere

from back then? Land records perhaps? Nondigital."

"Eh? I thought you were with the government. Surely Karma herself has it all."

"She doesn't," Hamilcar said. "Trust me, I need to go back to the old ways. Specifically, I want to question the previous owners of those properties that Dojo bought and sold."

"Hmm." The brigadier snuffed out his pipe. "You know, when the army digitized the last of our records, we sent all the books to the National Library. They've got acres of stuff underground. I wouldn't be surprised if the old land registries are down there too."

"The library," Hamilcar said. "Of course."

Chapter Twelve

Why the Generals Cried

"Why are we here?" Colonel Shakia hissed. "Karma specifically told us to drop this."

"She's got a blind spot," Hamilcar said. "I'm the fail-safe."

They were deep in the stacks, a hermetically sealed room that seemed somehow still choked with dust, under the watchful gaze of two ancient drones that trudged up and down on maglev rails, nightmarish many-armed things. As Colonel Shakia had already verified, they responded sluggishly to vocal commands, and their chief functions seemed to be fetch and carry, and fight fires.

The National Library proper, four stories above on ground level, was a high-ceilinged, swanky hall much like a cathedral, one of the wonders of the city, where tourists came to see ancient Buddhist and Hindu texts. The first three basements were archives, searchable through a manual interface. The last, fourth basement was a cavernous dumping ground filled with racks of material no one had even bothered to catalogue, let alone read, and it was clear from the logs that they were the first humans to enter here in the last seven years.

"We need an army to go through this," Colonel Shakia said, after they had wandered the aisles for half an hour.

Hamilcar stared at her. A look of amusement crept across his face.

"What?" She frowned, irritated.

"You are a colonel. You actually *have* an army."

An hour later, eighty-six of Kathmandu's fiercest weekend warriors were cheerfully gathered in the bowels of the National Library, clad in fatigues and combat helmets, tackling with bewildered gusto an enemy comprised of deeds, documents, registers, and irritable drones. This floor was not wired up to the Virtuality; to a certain degree, they had privacy, and Hamilcar's carte blanche was enough to ward off suspicious librarians.

Twelve exhausting hours later, they found it: original land registers, original title deeds from that time period, all packed in giant paper sacks marked "To Be Destroyed." Some conscientious bureaucrat had saved them, or more likely, no one had gotten around to them yet with a flamethrower. The fourth basement was full of "To Be Destroyed" sacks, most of them harmless paperwork long since transcribed into immortal databases, the detritus of a bygone era slowly settling to dust.

"The last time anyone actually owned property." Colonel Shakia held up the register ending on KD1. "Feels weird, thinking everyone owned little pieces of the city, like a quilt."

Hamilcar was scanning the papers, his eye twitching as the Echo took over some of its functionality. The augments allowed rapid absorption of data, even analog, although most humans no longer required data at all, other than for the sake of amusement. It made his eye twitch in an unpleasant way.

"There's something here," he said finally. "I've found eight of the deeds Doje purchased."

"I'm guessing all of the sellers are dead?" Colonel Shakia asked.

"Not even dead. They don't exist. There is no mention of them at all in the census on KD1."

"Erased? How is that even possible? Karma cannot be hacked. Not even Doje could have this much power," Colonel Shakia said.

"The only answer, then," Hamilcar said, "is that Karma already knows."

Colonel Shakia slumped back against a rack. Some of the vitality drained out of her face. "What now, then? Are we to fight Karma herself? We are alone in this."

Hamilcar smiled. "No, not alone."

"What are we going to do?"

"You head back to the tower and get ready. Me? I'm going to go make a wish."

~

He didn't hear Gurung coming. He certainly didn't see him. The first inkling he had was the smooth pull of the Gurkha's knife, the little whoosh it made as it left the scabbard, and a sharp cold edge pressed against his neck, a motion so fast that his brain had barely registered anything before he was on his knees on the gravel.

"I came to make a wish," Hamilcar said softly, trying to keep the blade from nicking his Adam's apple.

The knife eased up a bit.

"You're a company man," Gurung said, from somewhere behind him. "Karma's pet."

"I can still dream of wishes," Hamilcar said. "Is this not the Garden of Dreams, where the djinn grant wishes?"

"You can't see the djinn," Gurung said. "You tell me your wish, I decide if they hear it."

"This wish is for you to grant, Bhan Gurung."

The knife pressed back against his throat with alarming quickness.

"What game is this, Sheriff?"

"I want a wish from you."

"I am not a djinn."

"You are Bhan Gurung, the knife saint, champion of your regiment, who murdered twenty-three people in cold blood, sentenced to death in a secret military tribunal. You were guilty, beyond doubt, of the most violent crime in Kathmandu in a hundred years. I heard that the four judges at your trial wept to a man. Why did they weep, Gurung?"

"That's your wish?"

"Yes."

"To know why the generals cried?"

"Yes."

Gurung sighed. The knife moved away. Hamilcar touched his neck, half expecting his head to fall off. He sat back on the ground in relief, trying to still his shaking legs.

"You want some pistas?" Gurung sat down beside him, on a rock.

"Sure." He ate one and looked at the shell.

"I just throw the shells on the ground, it drives the girl djinn crazy." Gurung grinned. "Mister Sheriff, what will you do with an old story like that? There are no more generals left in the city, and no more tears, either. No one wants to know those old things."

"I came here, didn't I?"

"You are on Karma's side."

"I am Karma's failsafe. If she fails, it is my job to make it right. "

Gurung snorted. "Karma never fails. You are a straw man."

"So take a chance, Bhan Gurung. Let me count for something. Tell me why they cried."

"Fine," Gurung said. "It is a short story. Not remarkable. When I was tried, I admitted my guilt readily. As you said, there was no doubt. I was appointed a military lawyer, but I told him to stay home. At the tribunal, I waived my defense and accepted all of the prosecutor's evidence as truth. No cross-examination, no questions.

"Suspecting a ploy, they asked me if I would plead insanity, and I said no, I had been and was still perfectly sane. In fact I was willing to sign an affidavit to that effect. Puzzled, they asked finally if I would plead for leniency, given my exemplary record. I said no. I requested death by firing squad, at their earliest convenience. I then thanked them for their time, saluted, and stood down from the dock. It was done in ten minutes, the shortest trial in the history of the tribunal. Still they were not satisfied. As a parting shot, one of them held my collar and asked me why. Why, man, did you kill so many people?

"It was the first time anyone had asked why. I asked if they had time to hear a story. I assured them it would have no bearing on my plea or the verdict. They looked at each other, and, to a man, said yes.

"So I told them the story of the businessman Doje,

who was rich beyond measure. He bought cheap and sold high, isn't that business? He accrued great wealth doing this, and wasn't that a virtue? He sold people, also. It was the time when microclimate equilibrium was up for grabs, and PMDs were just getting started, so pretty soon it was obvious that if you had enough people, your city or town or whatever would win the nanotech battle. Survival. All of a sudden, cities *wanted* refugees, all those little rich communities that had walled themselves in, they realized they didn't have enough warm bodies to run their microclimes. The math was getting better, and the AIs could tell you to an exact number what population you needed to be viable. So, brokers like Doje started shifting migrants around, and when the spring ran dry, they started snatching them off the streets and *selling* them.

"It accelerated before KD1. He shifted five thousand in that last month alone, sold them to some failed town in America, and they all died a month later, because the numbers still weren't right. I guess he figured once Karma came online all of this would stop. Because he didn't give a shit, he did three thousand more, and this time there weren't enough people in the villages, so he just started grabbing them right here, off the streets. There were food riots already, no one in charge, it was easy."

"And the properties he bought?"

"Wartime profiteering," Gurung said. "It was win-win for him. He'd auction off some small landholder's entire family, take their house, fake the documentation, and then strike their name off the census altogether. Men, women, children, babies, grandmothers, uncles, aunts, he'd sell the whole lot, and take whatever they had. Double the profit. No one asked questions, people were moving around all the time, according to whim or rumor."

"Your family?"

"All gone. Sold. Thirty-two of them. Dead somewhere. My kaka, my oldest uncle, he didn't even make it out of the city, he died in the sky, they eventually dumped his body from the plane somewhere over the Kanchenjunga. I was gone in the army, they missed me somehow. Or maybe Doje didn't care. What could one man do, anyway, a simple soldier? That tower he asked for, that your Karma gave him? That used to be a two-story house before. Three bedrooms upstairs, and a big kitchen on the ground floor. Big wooden table from a single tree. You could fit a lot of people around it."

"Yours?"

Gurung looked at the ground.

"And now you've come back to tear it all down," Hamilcar said. "Everything bad and everything good. Just burn it all."

"Maybe I should have died. I wanted to. Karma even fucked that up," Gurung said.

"Maybe you should have," said Hamilcar Pande, failsafe.

Chapter Thirteen

Supper at the Tower of Gold

"Tonight, Lord of Tuesday, you shall become the God King of this city." Bhan Gurung's bow was particularly low and flourishy. In the Gurung lexicon of physical movements, which Melek Ahmar had taken to studying closely, this was especially menacing, as it presaged that he was about to embroil his master in something egregious.

With his mouth full of potatoes and yak steak, the djinn king was caught off guard, and by the time he had swallowed, the opportunity to run away was lost.

"Tonight, I am playing backgammon with ReGi," Melek Ahmar said with as much dignity as he could muster.

"No sir, tonight we are girding ourselves for momentous acts."

"Tonight I have the stomach ache . . ."

Gurung gave only a sidelong glance at the table, groaning under the scattered remnants of an entire yak plus the condiments, side dishes, sauces, narcotics, and unguents required to make said yak palatable, but it was enough to make his damnable point, and cause Melek Ahmar to retreat further into his routine of well-worn excuses. The damn Gurkha was a bully, there were no two ways about it, and to fend off his bland smile for long was exhausting.

"Look, Gurung, now is not the time for reckless acts, we are accruing karma at a fantastic clip, yes, thanks to your plan, and we should enjoy life, throw a party, bestow our munificence upon our flock . . ." Melek Ahmar said.

"Lord, I propose no reckless act."

"Ah, good, well, that's settled then." *I don't believe you. Every act you propose is reckless. You are the most unsatisfactory servant in the entire history of servitude.*

"In fact, all I propose is that we leave this garden, which, as charming as it is in its infinite variety, has been growing fetid and—"

"Fetid?"

"No doubt the combination of your magnificence combined with the dankness of the lady's herbs, but fetid, certainly. I simply propose we take a stroll outside, socialize with the city, pay a house call or two."

"Stroll where?"

"To the golden tower so visibly disturbing our sunsets."

"We are *not* attacking the tower," Melek Ahmar said. "I forbid it!"

"Attack? Why, Lord, we are welcomed guests there."

"What? The tower of your mortal enemy, the tower which you stare at for hours at a time while eating pistas and touching your knife in a suggestive way, that tower?"

Whereupon Bhan Gurung flourished a note handwritten on fancy paper and sealed with actual wax, which indeed included an invitation for supper at midnight, complete with a thoughtful list of pass codes to get past security. It was signed by one Hamilcar Pande.

"Who is he?"

"He is the sheriff, Karma's cat's-paw, the *failsafe*. A laughable concept, an eyewash position, but he is a man who thinks he can actually live up to his rank. He is too stupid to understand his role as a rubber stamp, and therefore dangerous in his own way, because he might do something unexpected, such as this. Karma has given him carte blanche, and he has invited us in. We will incur no karmic loss for what happens tonight."

"It's a trap."

"A trap is only effective if it can swallow its prey."

"Hmmphh. No power exists in this city which can swallow me." *You compel me to say these things, and I can see where this is going, Gurung, you bastard, I'll have no peace until that damn tower comes down. Damn the day I met you.*

So at eleven o'clock two djinn and one Bhan Gurung strolled down the street out of the garden, turned right on the boulevard and then left, past the flower shop, past a group of revelers at the garden bar, where they were recognized and had to decline many drinks, past the impromptu concert that had sprung up next to the wrought-iron bridge one street over, although ReGi lingered a few moments with a wistful look at the very handsome K-pop idol–looking fellow who was belting out hits, straddling the stage with a sweaty, showoffy look.

In any case, despite this dawdling, far too soon they were at the perimeter of the tower, girded for war, their intent unmistakable. He had a sledgehammer hastily ensorcelled with flashy blue light, not the Mace of One Hit, but really, that thing was a bit problematic at the best of times, what with hardly being able to lay it down without accidentally wrecking something, and people not appreciating impromptu craters and subsequently cursing him and spreading mean stories about him. No, the Hammer of Dawn was flashy and debonair and rather easier to use.

ReGi had her hand-rolled cigarette clamped martially between her lips, and assured him she had other weapons of immense proportion on her person, which, given her gothic black vampire cloak, could well be true. Gurung had his knife and that mad look in his eyes, which was enough.

The tower compound was walled, and the gate was predictably closed. Three fist-sized drones buzzed alertly, and started to converge on them as they slowed down. ReGi waved her hands and her distortion field sprang to life, vibrant and powerful like the wild forest she had nurtured in the alternate Garden of Dreams. The drones began to slow and list, as numerous things failed within them on a quantum level, and then ReGi did something to turn up the entropy within the field, so that they actually began to flake and rust and shear apart, aging visibly, until three very feeble, shortsighted drones persisted, following them in a querulous manner and emitting their aches and pains within electronic sighs.

Bhan Gurung, meanwhile, had tried the first of his passwords on a manual touchpad, and the gate slid open, granting them ingress onto a short graveled path, neatly raked by some mechanical gardener. Their footsteps crunched eerily on the pebbles as they approached the heavy double wooden doors, carved in dragon motifs.

"Allow me, please," Melek Ahmar said.

He swung his hammer and smashed it right into the center of the stupid dragon head. The effect was gratifying. The door simply disintegrated, wiping out several thousand bittos' worth of irreplaceable two-hundred-year-old wood carving. They stomped into a large, cool white entrance hall, marbled and empty, somewhat like a posh mausoleum.

"Halt," a voice chimed from all directions. Marble-sized drones emerged from recesses in the ceiling, a swarm of metal bees promising lethal kinetic force. "Rustic One and Two, and Lady of the Garden. You have been identified. Kindly cease and desist. This is Karma."

ReGi snapped her field on, and they were instantly covered in its eldritch shield. Melek Ahmar, as befitting a warrior king, stayed loose, the hammer dangling in a louche manner from his left hand. Everything was always being recorded in this era. One had to constantly strike glamorous poses.

"Karma the tyrant machine," he said. "You're here too? What luck."

"I am everywhere," Karma replied. "But yes, for tonight I am mostly here."

"Good, in that case I can mostly kill you, when I turn this place to rubble presently."

"I cannot be killed, Rustic One," Karma said. "But my algorithms predict that *you* can be, despite your lineage. I request you to leave the city, Rustic One. It is not my preference to harm you."

"I think we both know I'm not leaving," Melek Ahmar

said with a tiny hint of regret. He glared at Bhan Gurung, who himself was sauntering about with his typical rakish look. *The Red King does not walk away from fights with God-Machines. Am I that fucking easily manipulated? I've got to work on that...* "My name is Melek Ahmar, I am the Red King, the Lord of Tuesday, et cetera et cetera, I'm sure you've heard of me, and *even if you haven't*, I don't give a FUCK!"

He screamed because at just that moment the bee drones converged on him at supersonic speed, all intent on tearing out chunks from his body. Luckily ReGi had been paying attention. Her distortion field pulled the three of them back to back, and then turned opaque, a solid shield that crackled along the circumference with electrical discharge. The kinetic swarm converged and then bounced off the shield, pinballing around the room, smashing holes into the fine marble walls. After five minutes of admiring her handiwork, Melek Ahmar reached out with a massive wave of power, a concussive blast that simply turned all the drones to dust.

"I am disappointed that it has come to this," Karma said. "We charge you with willful destruction of city property and refusal to disperse. Colonel Shakia. You may take over defense of this tower and repel the hostiles."

"Certainly," Colonel Shakia replied smoothly, her

voice also echoing around the ruined hall. "Thank you, lady and gentlemen, for your demonstration. I am Colonel Shakia of Defense. Please note that I am now authorized to use lethal force. Consider this your last chance to retreat before I whip you like dogs and scour the skin off your backs."

"I want her head too," Melek Ahmar said.

"They're at the top," Gurung said, racing for the stairs.

The stairwell was broad and deep, a spiraling marble monstrosity that stretched up and up. ReGi groaned as they got to it.

"You want me to climb up all that way?"

Gurung grinned. "You're getting a bit pudgy, Lady Djinn, if you don't mind me saying so. Some stairs would be good for you."

ReGi scowled. Which was her normal expression, and thus failed to convey the sheer depth of her current sulk.

Melek Ahmar half expected the stairwell to be booby-trapped, as it would have been in the old days, with spikes and pits and hot oil falling from murder holes, but they were left alone until they got to the next floor. The double doors were wide open, and they could see the grand hallway filled with precious artifacts, all glittering with gold.

Colonel Shakia cared nothing for these things. A couple of large drones came out of the entrance, spewing liquid fire, barreling through a priceless statue from the ancient Pala civilization. Heat washed over them as they crouched beneath ReGi's spherical shield. Melek Ahmar laughed, because who attacks djinn with fire, after all, and then remembered that Gurung was perhaps not so fond of flames, and in any case this was some kind of unclean, phosphorous heat that was uncomfortable and possibly even harmful to him, and ReGi was sweating somewhat, so he stepped out of her sphere and charged the drones, his hammer flashing. They swiveled to face him, and in that moment's gap he shot out a fist of air, a primal extrusion of his field that bashed them against the wall. He struck with the Hammer of Dawn, reducing the drones into requisite parts.

After that, it was a running battle up the staircase, close quarters and nasty. On the third-floor landing, they got hit by liquid nitrogen and then some kind of EMP shockwaves, and on the fourth by some even older drones using projectile weapons. The enemy ranged from football-sized spheres to tiny machines the size of ants, but Melek Ahmar smashed through them all with only a few scrapes.

"This is easy!" he bellowed. "And fun! Finally a good fight!"

"It's not," ReGi said through gritted teeth.

"They're herding us," Gurung said. "Testing."

"Yup. Karma's watching our reactions to different attacks," ReGi said. "She's mapping our abilities."

Melek Ahmar frowned. "Tricky devil." *Good thing I have yet to reveal the full magnificence of my power. These idiots think I'm some chump with a hammer.*

"I thought we were invited," ReGi said.

"They're not all on the same page," Gurung said. "Something to exploit when we get to the top."

Antigravity was easy for ReGi to disrupt, and those state-of-the-art drones were murderously expensive, something Colonel Shakia had figured out, apparently, because she was now sending them very old, mechanical machines moving on gears, nightmare apparitions like attack horse-dogs that moved on four squat horse legs and carried a mouthful of nasties. Some of them had scorpion tails sprouting from their shoulder humps, with poisoned stingers. These were problematic; they used momentum to get through the distortion field, and their internal mechanisms were somehow more resistant to many of ReGi's tricks.

Melek Ahmar drew his field in, reducing it to a millimeter-thick skin, harder than tungsten, harder, indeed, than any metal known to man, for he had once walked through dragon flame like this, through the core fire at the center of the Earth. This was one of his specialties, they used to call him Ahmar Steelskin in the old days, even the fabled lance of Kuriken had blunted against his chest. Of course, that stupid Homer had stolen his story and fame and given it to puny Achilles, and then woven a great boring poem around it. There was a case pending about that in the djinn courts.

He motioned the others back and let the first three horse-dogs converge on him, laughed as their stings and mouth spikes bounced off his armor. He brought the hammer down on one head, smashed it to bits, and then frowned as the thing kept on going undeterred. Two others now had his arms, and were trying to drag him down. Gurung darted out of one side, ridiculously brave, and somehow his knife plunged into some weak spot near the abdomen of the damaged hound, a quick, effortless stab through steel that made the horse-dog keel over and lie kicking on the stairs like a butchered animal, unable to regain its feet.

"Gyroscope," Gurung said, hastily retreating behind ReGi's shield. "Nothing in the heads. Their brain is in their stomach."

A healthy Melek Ahmar possessed a terrible strength, wholly unrelated to his disruption field. He raised his arms above his head and lifted his attackers straight off the ground, and as they scrambled in the air he smashed them together repeatedly, until parts started flying off and they made whining machine yelps that sounded peculiarly like actual dogs in distress.

Onward and upward, in an orgy of violence and lit-tered parts, oil and metal, and now and then blood, as they took small nicks and cuts. The sheer volume and di-versity of weaponry at Colonel Shakia's disposal slowed them down, until even Melek Ahmar's enthusiasm began to wane. After an interminable trek they reached the penultimate floor, where the walls were actually curved up, the tip of the tower narrowing considerably along the way, the stairwell itself becoming much tighter, no longer marble but a functional steel, and it was apparent that the next floor up had only one room at the very apex. Here the doors were thick, shining metal, obviously impene-trable, and as they approached the landing, they heard movement behind them, and a portion of the stairwell smoothly receded, leaving them stranded. Here at last they were at the chokepoint, a killing field prepared lov-ingly by Colonel Shakia and her mistress Karma.

"As much as I have enjoyed our game, I must ask you now to surrender," Colonel Shakia said, her voice echoing around. "The door ahead is impenetrable, even for you, Rustic One. You are, in fact, in a metal box. Karma has ana-lyzed your powers and prepared a variety and scale of drone attack which has currently a sixty-eight percent chance of penetrating your defenses. This percentage will go up as we test you further. You will fall in the end, djinn or not."

Melek Ahmar bared his teeth. *At last, a worthy adversary.* "I piss on your sixty-eight percent. I am the djinn king Melek Ahmar, One of Seven. You have analyzed only a tithe of my strength. I can reduce this entire tower to dust."

"Then we are at an impasse," Colonel Shakia said. "Karma has prepared even for this eventuality. Should you unleash the full potential of your power, I am authorized to release the Q bomb. I am unable to explain the exact physics of it, but its main function is to reset all quantum states within a radius, essentially scrambling the area into a primordial soup. I am assured that even your so called 'distortion effect,' which relies on a type of exotic field of non-baryonic nature, possibly—even such a thing might be disrupted, although we lack the data to simulate its precise manner. Karma now posits that your field might be the overlay of a ghost universe, a previous iteration of our current state, a sad remnant, which would make you partial ghosts, relics of a dead distant past. I digress. Your choices are clear. Either leave the city, or we all die a very unusual death. Frankly, I'm bored with this whole thing so I implore you to decide quickly."

"Bored?" Melek Ahmar roared. "Bored?!"

"Or a third option," Gurung said with a wink. "We open the door."

He put his palm flat on the door and murmured an incantation and like open sesame the metal slabs slid apart.

Chapter Fourteen

Keys to God

Hamilcar Pande reclined on a terribly expensive couch in Doje's inner sanctum, feet up on a mahogany coffee table, almost dozing off, ignoring for the most part the cat-and-mouse of the drone versus djinn combat. The previously austere room had been turned hastily into a control center, the air inside tense and disturbed. The old man sat in front of a 3-D holographic battle feed, exhorting his mechanical forces and offering a disbelieving commentary on the state of affairs. Apparently fending off attacks by a fat djinn and a little girl djinn had not been high on his list of possible things to do this week.

The Mongolian Mr. Khunbish sat behind, strapped in combat armor, eyes closed in silent meditation. He was a pacifist of sorts and required a Zen-like state to initiate any kind of violence. Colonel Shakia was ensconced in a command module plugged in directly to Karma, her head encased in a liquid gel helmet that greatly enhanced her mental reflexes, permitting her to command multiple drones without burning out her Echo with excessive data flow. She was, of course, the only one doing anything useful; her body was sheathed in sweat, and various muscles were twitching.

The last occupant of the room was Karma, several full tiers of her mind focused on this event, crunching numbers against the djinn's distortion fields, and her presence was almost a physical thing, a ghost floating above, giving them all a peculiar sense of safety. The God-Machine was *in* the room. What could go wrong?

So when the doors slid open, they all looked up, aghast, except for Hamilcar Pande, who lounged in his chair and smiled in greeting.

"The *door*!" Doje shouted, staring up at the domed roof, where presumably he expected to find Karma floating in the ether. "The *fucking impenetrable door* opened!"

"Good evening, Doje," Gurung said. He stepped in front of the djinn, and the two old men stared at each other, men whose shared history had brought the city to this moment of gibbering madness, this potential collision of ghost universes and quantum undoing.

"What is the meaning of this, Sheriff?" Karma's voice floated down from above, like an irritated goddess. "You have betrayed us."

"I invited them," Hamilcar Pande said. "Respectfully, Karma, you asked me to find another way. Frankly speaking, I had no desire to send my beloved Kanelia into an assault on the garden. I'm very fond of the garden."

"Thank you," ReGi said with a curtsey.

Colonel Shakia made a strangled noise from inside her gel helmet, disavowing any such love.

"Furthermore," Hamilcar Pande said, "the weapons you are seeking to use, well, it seems like they could unravel a whole lot more than just this tower. Cocooned in this paradise, we think we are alone in this world, but that's not true, is it? The planet has its share of hells. Who knows what will come out in response to a full unveiling of force? Escalation is not a good thing, is it, Karma? Is this not why some part of you gave me carte blanche?"

"Continue, Sheriff," Karma said after a moment. Her tone was icy, clinical.

Hamilcar Pande turned to the djinn. "Melek Ahmar, Lord of Tuesday, the Red King, are you amenable to terms we—"

"No, I'm fucking not!" Melek Ahmar roared. "I came here to rule! Either I sit on a throne tonight or I'm burning everything down!"

"Your karma score has been skyrocketing at an insane pace; pretty soon you might actually *warrant* a throne," Hamilcar Pande said with some amusement. "Although the wishes you're granting . . . gah, I can't imagine that's enjoyable."

"Bloody Gurung making me do the most unspeakable things, forcing me into continuous vile acts. Let me tell you, Sheriff, your bloody Humes think up the most ridiculous, horrible things to wish for, and then I'm forced to go out and grant them, and then all of you bastards sit around calling me names! I'm not having it anymore, I'm sick to death of this city, I wish I'd never come here!"

"I fail to see your strategy," Karma subvocaled to Hamilcar. *"Rustic One appears unstable. You are upsetting him. He possesses enormous destructive energy, and possibly the mind of an imbecile. You are risking our survival."*

"Our survival? The survival of the city is paramount. You and I are not synonymous with the city."

"I see."

"I am the failsafe. Have you failed, Karma?"

"You are arrogant, Sheriff. You presume too much. I have chosen wrongly to put my faith in you."

"Perhaps. Nonetheless, I will see this through. Do you agree?"

"I see no better option at this moment."

"Noble Mars," Hamilcar Pande said. "You are a true and ancient king of the Djinndom, one of seven, correct?"

"One of Seven," Melek Ahmar confirmed. "That's what I've been saying. Do you think us djinn just fling around kingships like you Humes?"

"Is delivering justice not one of the duties of the king?"

"Do you in fact acknowledge me as the king of this demesne?" A crafty gleam lit up Melek Ahmar's face. "Djinn follow exacting laws and documentation, you know." He snapped his finger. "ReGi! I take it you are well versed in drawing up contracts? This here Hume is offering us a throne . . ."

"Let us say you are more akin to a visiting judge," Hamilcar Pande said. "A dignitary, hmm? A most valued monarch come here on a royal tour, humbling us with your wisdom and legalese. In this, Karma and I speak as one, and we apologize for the paucity of our welcome."

"Well said, Sheriff." Melek Ahmar smiled expansively. "Finally, the courtesy owed between brother kings. I accept your invitation. I must say, your reception has been lacking somewhat."

"I was speaking of justice," Hamilcar Pande said. "I am the investigator. Perhaps you would deign to hear my case."

"Justice!" Doje shouted. "The sheriff speaks true! I demand justice, Djinn King! Your servant Gurung has been hounding me for years. He almost killed me forty years ago, and now he has returned to finish the job! He has duped you into doing his bidding, King of Mars. He has brought you here to murder me!"

Melek Ahmar stared balefully at Gurung. "Is this true, Gurung?"

"Assuredly," Gurung said. He twirled his moustache and patted his knife.

"There you go," Melek Ahmar said. "We are indeed here to murder you. Sheriff, be a good fellow and hand him over. Perhaps cutting him up will put Gurung here in a good mood, and we can finally go back to throwing parties and enjoying ourselves."

"He confesses to wanting murder!" Doje said. "We are a city of laws, Djinn King. We value human life. We value fairness. These are the laws of Karma. You and your dogs have no place here."

"Yes, human life. Laws. Fair value," Hamilcar Pande said smoothly. "These are indeed the ideals we live by. Bhan Gurung, unfortunately, I cannot hand Doje over to you. Allow me to build my case in his defense. Do you in fact recall killing twenty-three men and women some forty years back, in an apparent attempt to murder this man, Doje?"

"Yes, I do," Gurung said.

"And did you torture and kill his brother during this episode?"

"I did."

"Why?"

"I was trying to find Doje," Gurung said.

"My poor brother," Doje wept.

"Bhan Gurung, did you almost kill Doje, when he finally returned home?"

"I did. I almost died myself."

"And then?"

"I was tried by the army and sentenced to death. My firing squad was set by some luck for what became KD1. Karma announced general amnesty and I was saved."

"Who set the date of your execution, Gurung?"

"The men who tried me."

"Who were?"

"I am not permitted to reveal the details of a military court to civilians." Gurung glanced around.

"I am Colonel Shakia, of Defense, I am the ranking military officer here," Kanelia Shakia said. Her gel helmet had receded into the cowl at the back of her chair, leaving a thin blue residue over her face, making her look vaguely aquatic. "I have the authority to declassify all records pertaining to your case, Gurung."

"There were four generals present in the room, and the recorder," Bhan Gurung said.

"I have the names of these generals," Hamilcar Pande said. "One of them, in particular, is interesting. His brother was the speaker of the house in parliament."

"That was hardly unusual, they're all corrupt and connected," Doje said. "The old system. Rotten to the core."

"Was it General SK Thapa who sentenced you?"

"Yes. I requested the firing squad," Gurung said. "He selected the date, as the head of the tribunal."

"Curious, isn't it, that he should pick the exact date of KD1," Hamilcar said. "A man such as him, so well connected, he would surely know in advance the day for Karma to assume power. It is almost as if he deliberately picked a day on which he knew no execution could occur."

Gurung looked stricken. This thought had clearly never occurred to him.

"So, some attempt was perhaps made to preserve your life," Hamilcar continued. "Can you think why?"

"I cannot." Gurung stared at Doje.

"Throughout this investigation, one thing disturbed me ... Why?" Hamilcar said. "So many whys. Why, for example, did Doje buy so many properties before KD1? Why did Karma give him so many points for them?"

"I am not under investigation, Sheriff!" Doje snapped.

"So many whys. Why did the generals cry? Why did Thapa save Gurung's life?" Hamilcar ignored the old man. "Gurung's crime was clear for all to see. There was nothing to investigate there. What was not clear was Doje's crime. Not wanting to waste Karma's abundant faith in me, I chose to investigate precisely that."

"Karma!" Doje snarled. "I requisition the immediate

termination of this murderer noncitizen Gurung! And that the traitor Hamilcar Pande be stripped of his citizenship and executed!"

"Not right now," Karma said.

"I demand it, damn you! You're supposed to serve us! I have your fucking karma points! I'm cashing them in, damn you, do as I say!"

"Your request must be postponed," Hamilcar Pande said smoothly. "We are in an external emergency. After this is resolved, by all means we will submit to Karma's calculations."

"You lie!"

"Such an agreement is amenable, Sheriff," Karma said. "Please note that the extraordinary leeway given to you ends here. Pending this inquiry, we will honor esteemed Doje's request in exchange for his points."

"What? *All of my points?*" Doje asked, aghast.

"You are asking for the death of two men, one of whom is my sheriff," Karma replied. "It will be your last request."

"Fine! Fuck you. You think I exist only in this place? You think I put all my eggs in your fucking karmic-point basket? Take them and kill the dogs."

"We are aware of everything, esteemed Doje," Karma said.

"How elegant your equations are, Karma," Hamilcar

said. "You dispose of all three of us with one stroke. It seems I have signed my own sentence." He glanced at Kanelia. She was sitting rigid, her face unreadable. He hoped fervently that she wouldn't draw her gun and end everything right now. "Well, it seems as if my investigation was useless after all. I suppose there's no place in this world for men like us anyway."

"I am curious," ReGi, the Lady of the Garden, said. "What was your answer? Why did Gurung try to kill Doje?"

"Yes, I too am curious," Melek Ahmar rumbled.

"Doje's game was the selling of people. Climate refugees, force-fitted with PMDs and sold off to the highest bidder, necessary to produce microclimates for towns and cities without enough people," Hamilcar said. "Almost twenty thousand people trafficked in two months alone, preceding KD1. But Doje was not a mere trafficker, no. In the end he started also confiscating properties around town, using false sales deeds, which we have gathered from the National Library archives. Funny thing, that, all the digital data was triple scrubbed, but he forgot about the handwritten stuff altogether. It was just lying there, with the land registers. And those poor fools sold off, their properties taken? Well, they don't appear on the census. Karma. Why don't they appear on your census at all?"

"Twenty thousand, eh?" Doje was relaxed now, his face losing the mask of a dignified old man and assuming a more natural, reptilian cast. "It was closer to twenty-five. I sold whole villages, Sheriff, whole fucking villages. Easiest money I ever made. I even had my own airstrip. And the PMDs? They were doctored. If you dial them all the way up, you can turn a human body into a nanotech factory. Every other biochemical process slows down, and of course you don't live as long, but hell, it's the cheapest way to jump-start a microclime. Turns the people into drooling brainless lumps of meat, though. Climate jacking, they called it. There are cities on the map that wouldn't exist without people like me."

"And you got paid handsomely, got paid twice, in fact, first by your buyers and then by Karma," Hamilcar said. "And she even covered it up for you. Why, Karma?"

Karma did not answer.

"Covered it up?" Doje laughed. "You think I did all that by myself? *Karma fucking told me to do it!*"

"What?" Hamilcar went limp as half his feed went blind. His Echo blinked, and then scrambled like a drowning man trying to find purchase. *I can't see the data. She's cut me off from the Virtuality.*

"About a hundred thousand too many people in the valley," Doje drawled. "They were all pouring in from the countryside, too, clogging up the city. Poor, stupid Sheriff. You should have stayed Karma's errand boy. Wrong time to grow a spine. Before KD1, Karma handed out *orders*. This many people in paradise, and no more. And someone had to be the sweeper, clean out the gutters. Guess what? It paid to be the sweeper. You're a Pande, aren't you? One of your own did it too. You think I was the only one cleaning house for her? I know every fucking dirty secret. I'm a fucking civic pillar, I'll crack this city in half before I go down."

"Sheriff," Karma said, her voice booming from the ceiling. "You are close to having a heart attack."

Bile rose in the back of Hamilcar's throat. *Can she do that? Are there backdoors in the PMD? Of course there are . . .* He tried to speak, but nothing came out, just his Echo muttering like a demented ape. He fell to his knees, hands twitching, trying desperately to swivel his head toward Kanelia, his body splaying in different directions.

"Nothing more to say, Sheriff?" Doje asked mockingly. "I guess the investigation is over. I will now collect my boon. Mr. Khunbish, if you would kindly execute the traitors?"

Chapter Fifteen

Knife Saint

The giant Mongolian stepped forward almost reluctantly, his combat suit making a swishing sound with each stride. Colonel Shakia tried to get out of her command chair and inexplicably found her arms and legs turning to mush, as her own PMD reacted to the sudden, full onslaught of Karma's electronic assault. Hamilcar watched her military-grade nervous system try to shrug it off and then the shadow of the Mongolian fell over him.

He raised his hand and half caught the armor-powered fist. It smashed through his wrist, splintering it, and even then the blow to his collar bone was heavy enough to break it, folding his body in two. A titanium-booted foot stomped on his knee, effectively wrecking it, leaving him twitching like a half-crushed insect pinned to a board.

His PMD was reacting like a groggy alcoholic, flooding his body with painkillers and adrenaline, while at the same time dealing very ineffectively with whatever viral weapons Karma had rained on it. *I should have got the upgrades.*

Mr. Khunbish was not a cruel man. He reached down and almost gently cradled Hamilcar's head between his hands, a deft touch despite the armor, and the servo motors in the suit hummed, a prelude to the vise that would no doubt pulp his skull. Half hanging from the Mongolian's grip, Hamilcar saw Kanelia marshal her unruly limbs. The ancient-looking revolver bloomed in her hand, blessedly free from electronics, momentarily immune to whatever Karma was hitting them with.

The gun fired, once, twice, and then she emptied the chambers. The noise was crazy loud, Hamilcar could hear it even through the metal hands encasing his head. The large-caliber bullets hit the Mongolian at point-blank range, and the giant warrior flinched back, even his battle suit not immune to the sheer kinetic power of mid-twenty-first-century lethality.

Kanelia threw the gun away and leapt over Hamilcar, not a wobble on her, the instinctive need to gore a momentarily stunned opponent driving her forward, muscle memory stamped into her body from her cage-fighting days. Her knife appeared in her left hand and she went low under the armpit for a sleeve joint, well aware of battle suits and their foibles.

Mr. Khunbish kicked her off with brutal power, and she landed on her back a few meters away. Very deliberately, she got to her feet and dusted herself off. She glanced once at Hamilcar, but he could see almost no recognition in her eyes, just an incandescent rage.

"Stand down, Colonel Shakia, this is an order," Doje said.

"I take no orders from you, fucker," she spat out. Her knife made a lazy orbit from Mr. Khunbish to Doje.

"Now, now, that's a mouth on you," Doje smiled. "Karma?"

"Stand down, Colonel Shakia," Karma said. Her words had a palpable gravity, as if the very pores of the room were filled with her substance. If she hadn't been fully engaged before, it was clear that the entirety of her mind was here now, focused on this one moment.

"Fuck off," the colonel snarled.

This time her head snapped straight up, and she went rigid. The PMD was a dumb mule, meant to resist outside influence. The Echo was a different kind of beast. Karma hit her with a psychic blast of data that Hamilcar could feel from meters away, a roaring river that would have swept away a lesser mind. Kanelia Shakia resisted for half a second, a lone fisher standing against the tsunami, and then finally, reluctantly, slid to one knee. Her knife fell from nerveless fingers.

Doje stepped over and slapped her across the face, hard enough to make blood gout from her split lips. The terrible old man picked up the knife, and Hamilcar watched in sickened panic, unable to look away.

"Oh, for fuck's sake." ReGi poked the djinn king in the back. "Fucking do something."

"Fucking stop!" Melek Ahmar shouted, raising one hand.

His power billowed out of him, almost a visible wave, and for the first time in his life Hamilcar Pande saw and felt the force of an elder djinn. If Karma's assault had been a gale, this was a nova, a roiling expansion of forces beyond the ken of human understanding. Time itself slowed into a trickle; movement was impossible, the air solidified, he could almost see the sonic ripple of Melek Ahmar's shouted command, waves in the dust. *We are flies in amber. What manner of creature is this? We have severely underestimated Rustic One . . . Karma, you're a fool to have let him in.*

Karma came back online, because she existed everywhere, but even her voice was tinny and weak, emanating from a single drone just out of the distortion field.

"Melek Ahmar, stand down, this does not concern you," Karma said. "Lest I deploy forces beyond even your control."

"You'll do fuck all," Melek Ahmar said. "I am the Eater of Worlds. Try me, I beg you."

"This *does not concern you.*" *Could a machine sound exasperated?*

The Lady ReGi came up behind the djinn king, almost swimming through the gelid air with exaggerated motions. Somehow she had rolled and lit a lopsided cigarette, and in between rather ineffective puffs, she whispered in his ear. Hamilcar felt a slight loosening of the pressure around his chest, and his ears popped, as time and space released their rictus grin. Pain came flooding back to his body. Melek Ahmar listened and frowned, then nodded, then looked around shrewdly, and then finally smiled.

"Karma!" His voice boomed up to the steeple. "I have a wager for you."

"What?"

"A wager. A bet. We djinn love a good bet. Are you in?"

"Do I have a choice?" Karma somehow managed to sound tart and irritable through her one distant mouthpiece.

"Your champion over there versus mine. Duel, one on one. No fancy stuff, just blood and guts fighting to the death. The old way, you know?"

"Am I to understand you are in the corner of my traitorous sheriff?"

"Yes, we like turncoats, we do," Melek Ahmar said. "Especially ones who betray kings. Funny thing, that, djinn don't actually like kings much. Damned interfering high and mighty bastards, I'd get rid of the lot of them . . .

We invented republicanism, did ya know that?"

"But . . . but you're a . . ."

"Right, right, King of Mars, One of Seven, so on, but well, there you go. Life is full of ironies. Still, that's ReGi's bet. And if you knew how much she can nag and pester, well, it's just easier to go along with it. Your man versus ours. Your big fella wins, we go away forever."

"And if the traitor wins?" Karma asks.

"One boon for each of us, you cannot refuse," ReGi said. "Anything we want, and no retaliation later on down the road. We get emissary status for life, yours or ours, whichever lasts longer. Contracts signed both here and with the Celestial Courts of the Djinn."

"Fine, I agree, provided your wishes do not harm my core programming," Karma said. "Release your field and I will restore functionality to the colonel and the sheriff. Although they appear slightly the worse for wear. I cannot help that."

Melek Ahmar sucked back his power, and normal physics returned with a hesitancy that showed it had been well and truly spanked and was now not nearly as smugly certain of its seat at the table. Hamilcar lifted his head up, noticing in a detached way that his right hand was dangling most curiously from the end of his broken wrist.

Colonel Shakia got to her feet and spat blood. She

lurched over to the djinn. "Thanks. I got this."

Bhan Gurung smiled. "No, Colonel saab, rest. *I've got this.*"

She stared at the old man. "You have no augments. He's in a fucking battle suit."

Gurung tapped his head. "No Echo. No PMD. Nothing to go awry at the critical moment. You trust Karma? I wasn't the one weeping blood when she turned up her juice."

Colonel Shakia sighed. "Armpit and back of the knee. Don't bother with the head, it's a solid piece. Take my knife, it's poisoned."

"So is mine, Colonel sir."

ReGi pushed up and kissed the Gurkha's leathery cheek. "Good luck, Uncle Gurung. You're a little bit scary, but I love you all the same."

Gurung looked at her a bit confused, and then handed her a packet. "Just hold these for a minute."

"What the hell is it?" Colonel Shakia asked.

"This?" ReGi shook the bag. "Pistachios, I think."

Gurung didn't swagger so much as slink his way toward the center mat, so casual that his knife wasn't even out yet when Mr. Khunbish swung for him. Gurung wasn't there. When the Mongolian straightened, his arm piece fell off, cut through along some invisible joint. Gurung smiled. Mr. Khunbish bulled forward for a double leg, an old wrestling move. Gurung flitted around, took one knee first and then the next, somehow appearing behind the armored giant. More pieces of hardware fell off. Two more passes, and Gurung was untouched, not even sweating, but his kukri was sweating blood, and there were deep furrows on the Mongolian's exposed limbs, cuts that dripped dark blue liquid.

Khunbish, aware now his armor was useless, stripped off his helmet and paused for a second, bellowing hard.

"He's sixty years old, for god's sake, just kill the fucker!" Doje shouted. There was a manic look on his face, fear seeping in now, as the old specter of Gurung rose once again before him, all too real and much too close.

Mr. Khunbish dropped his chest plate to the ground. He clapped his hands together and the electric eel nodes along his spine burst to life, enveloping him in a nimbus of blue light. He advanced in a classic Muay Thai stance, a flaming blue giant, foot snapping out in a teep, the front push kick used like a jab, followed by a series of heavy knees and elbows, looking for the fatal grapple. Gurung stepped into this flurry of blows, unafraid, took the battering and slid into the giant's reach, into the Thai plum, the Muay Thai neck clinch, and as those burning hands grasped him, as the stench of seared flesh wafted up, he wriggled his knife and slipped away, leaving a flaming carcass, a body slowly toppling over, throat sliced open, neck sawed in half and hanging by a gristle. Mr. Khunbish gave a strangled cry and died.

Gurung smiled, his face and body burned, cloth and skin flaking off. He reached over and wrenched the Mongolian's head off, placing it upright gently on the floor. Then he twirled his moustache with one bloody hand, turning the tips red.

"Lucky day, Karma," he said. "Two for one today."

"Karma! Karma!" Doje screamed, as Bhan Gurung walked him down.

No one stopped him. Karma didn't say a word

Chapter Sixteen

Boons from the God-Machine

"It was never my intention to kill you," Karma said to Hamilcar Pande. He was propped up in the command module, his broken body encased in a medical gel the chair itself had extruded. The rest of them were seated around him, a rough semicircle of bloodied victors.

Hamilcar Pande snorted. "You sold a hundred thousand people to microclime slavery."

"Doje misrepresented the case," Karma said. "In the Original Pact, I merely laid down conditions under which the conversion of the city would be successful. It was mathematics. My calculations indicated optimal conditions for the project. The choice was given to the leaders of the city. This was one of seven cities under consideration. I did not recommend any course of action. The algorithm simply indicated there were too many people. It was not optimal. It was the choice of you humans, Sheriff, your own parents and grandparents, to remove the unnecessary people. If you find the choice distressing, remember it is people who made it."

"You are not conscious. You have no preference."

"Precisely, Sheriff," Karma said.

"Unnecessary people," Colonel Shakia said, her face hard. "Some guy will always make that choice."

"Yeah. Humes always kill each other, nothing new. You owe us boons, Karma," ReGi said. "Pay up."

"Yes," Karma said. "One boon each. Then the three of you leave, forever. That is my condition. Ask, Lady of the Garden."

"I think Uncle Gurung ought to go first."

"I do not think he deserves a boon," Karma said. "He is sitting next to two heads which he has cut off, one of whom is my number six, Doje."

"You made a bet and lost, Karma," ReGi said. "Be a good sport."

"Fine," the God-Machine said. "Ask, Bhan Gurung."

"I got what I came for." Bhan Gurung patted the heads next to him.

"Am I to understand you want nothing more, and will hereafter leave our city in peace?" Karma asked.

"Wait. Him. Hamilcar. I want him to be the sheriff. For real. For life."

"What?" Karma asked.

"You need a failsafe, Karma," Bhan Gurung said. "He's a good failsafe. Make it for real. Make him real."

"And what precise role are you envisaging for Mr. Pande?" Karma asked.

"I don't know. He'll be your conscience. He knows what to do. Let him write his own chit. That's my boon."

"Granted. Sheriff, you are now hereby real, at the request of Bhan Gurung. And you will never return here, Gurung?"

"I believe I have what I came for."

"Lady?" Karma asked.

"The garden. I'm taking it."

"What?"

"You said I can't come back, so I'm going to take the garden. I've tended it all this time, it's mine. I'm going to put it in a snow globe."

"And what exactly will remain there once you *remove* it?"

"I dunno. Like a smoking ruin maybe? Oooh, maybe a black hole. Or one of those ghost universes you were talking about. Anyway, that's your problem, since you don't want me to come back or anything . . ."

"Fine, fine, am I to understand that if I permit you to stay here, you will consider *not* removing the Garden of Dreams from existence?"

"You have to give it to me," ReGi said. "Like my own fiefdom. I want to be the Duchess of the Garden. And you can't come in, not with any drones or surveillance or anything. One hundred percent privacy for me and my people."

"I will give you a ninety-nine-year lease. There is no private property in the city. This will be the first and only case, kindly do not bandy it about."

"And the duchess thing?"

"Fine, I will grant you the title of Duchess of the Garden, which will be purely ceremonial and—"

"Yay!"

"And you, sir, the Lord of Tuesday," Karma said finally. "Do you still wish to rule the city? For I am sorely tempted to hand it all over to you and take my talents somewhere without duchesses and Gurungs."

"No, no, that won't be necessary," Melek Ahmar said hastily. "Good luck with your new duchess and your fail-safe and er, that ferocious army lady. Me and Gurung are going to hit the road. Big wide world to see, eh? Been asleep for too long, and Gurung here's been lusting after vengeance all this time. We need to live! To explore! To fornicate! All too soon, the troubadours will sing once again of Melek Ahmar the Red King and his trusty lieutenant Bhan Gurung the Taker of Heads, they will talk of the day Melek Ahmar climbed ninety-nine flights of stairs, up the tower of doom, fighting alien hordes . . ."

"Is there a boon anywhere in this story?" Karma asked. For a machine, she was becoming terribly sarcastic, Hamilcar thought.

Melek Ahmar smiled a sly smile, and for a moment, the sheriff remembered how this goat-wearing rustic had somehow turned the city upside down.

"Karma, I want you to reset the counters," the Lord of Tuesday said. "Zeroes. I want everyone to be a zero."

"Why?" Karma asked, aghast. "Why?"

"What, I like zeroes," Melek Ahmar said. "They know how to party."

Chapter Seventeen

The End

On Karma Day 11,633, everyone in the city woke up a zero.

About the Author

Photograph courtesy of the author

SAAD Z. HOSSAIN is the author of two novels, *Escape from Baghdad!* and *Djinn City*. He lives in Dhaka, Bangladesh.

TOR·COM

Science fiction. Fantasy. The universe.

And related subjects.

*

More than just a publisher's website, *Tor.com*

is a venue for **original fiction, comics,** and

discussion of the entire field of SF and fantasy,

in all media and from all sources. Visit our site

today—and join the conversation yourself.

39492317R00100